I0831521

Revelations

Kristen Dovnik

This is a work of fiction. Names, characters, places, and incidents either are the product of the author's imagination or are used fictitiously. Any resemblance to actual persons, living or dead, events, or locales is entirely coincidental.

First Edition

Cover Design: Kristen Dovnik
Editor: Kim Campbell

Paperback ISBN: 978-0-6489540-8-8

Hardcover ISBN: 978-0-6489540-9-5

This book is for

the love of my life

my husband, my Robby.

Books by Kristen Dovnik

<u>The Chronicles of the Light Princess</u>

Conflictus

Contentment

HIGHLANDS
FAIRWIND FOREST
CASTLE RAE
MEADOWS
ODEGA
THE SWAY

1

I hang my head as I step out into the courtyard. It's eerily quiet while everyone walks out of the grand foyer and into the vast space. It's the day after the full moon and there is to be another public hanging. This has been happening on the regular as the Kings brother's soldiers fight their way towards the throne.

Long before I was born, Stephan, the Kings younger brother believed that he should rule, not his older brother, Roger. He managed to persuade a few men and women of the Sway to join his ranks in the hopes of moving up in the world. It has been a constant battle between us and them, and it seems as of late to only be getting worse.

In a little over three months, the Princess will come of age and Roger will be forced to step down so she may assume the throne. Princess Hayley is exactly like her father. She is nasty and cruel, especially behind closed doors. I honestly don't want to be stuck under her rule. Who knows what new laws she will impose upon our people?

The courtyard is overly crowded today as we all gather around the gallows. I see my beloved Joshua standing off to the side with the other King's guards and make my way over. I walk around a woman holding a baby and step to the side to allow a man with a crooked leg to walk past. Joshua eye's me as I get closer and moves slightly to the left to allow me to stand beside him.

"Why are there so many people here today? It's unusual for there to be a crowd this size." I ask, looking around as I notice that the royals haven't arrived yet. That doesn't surprise me though, they love being fashionably late.

"We are hanging Duke Stephan's second in charge," Joshua whispers as a matter of fact while never taking his eyes off the crowd. His brown hair hangs loosely over his eyes, and he shakes his head to the side, moving it out of the way. The soldier on his left bumps his shoulder into Joshua's and signals with his head towards the gallows.

There is a man with a hood over his head. Suspiciously, he looks around before quickly moving away from the tall wooden beams. "Go check it out." Joshua commands and the guard steps away.

My heart is beating erratically in my chest as I watch the guard walk towards the gallows. Even on such a dreadful day, the towns women still swoon or even try to flirt with the passing guard. He ignores them as he passes by and begins to inspect where the man was standing.

He looks around for a while before his eyes go wide and he drops himself out of sight. I hold my breath; sensing Joshua is too. There hasn't been an attack on the castle for quite a long time. If we really are hanging someone of importance to the rebels, I do not doubt that they would try something today.

After a few agonising moments, the guard becomes visible, looks directly at Joshua, and shakes his head. Thankfully, it's nothing.

The trumpets sound and everyone begins to bow down as the King and Queen enter the courtyard, taking their seats upon their thrones. For a moment I'm startled to see that Princess Hayley is not with them; but then a single trumpet begins to sound. I glance at the Queen and notice the very slight shake of her head as her daughter makes her entrance. She's disappointed in her daughter's need to always be important. Today is not about her. It is about the King showing his dominance over those wishing to kill him; and her for that matter. Maybe the day is about her too.

The Queen raises her head, and we lock eyes for only a moment before she turns away. I see a small smile play out on her lips, which makes me smile in return. I may be one of her ladies' maids, but it warms my heart to see her like that. She is kind and gentle towards me. She always has been, just like she was my mother. I used to play in her drawing room as a child while my mother got her ready for the extravagant balls Castle Rae used to host. Many of my childhood memories have her in them. I cherish them even more now since my mother passed away.

"Are you alright?" Joshua asks quietly, as he peers down over his shoulder before refacing the crowd. He locks eyes with a soldier along the opposing wall and gestures towards the crowd. The guard breaks rank and begins to patrol the perimeter. Everyone is on edge although no one is willing to show it, especially with the King perched up there on his throne.

"Yes and no, you know how I hate these things," I say as I rub my hand up and down my arm. These sorts of situations make me so uncomfortable. You never know when someone or something is going to jump out and attack. They did that so many times in the beginning when the King conducted the first trials.

"That I do, but you know why the King is doing this." He states while never taking his eyes off his duty.

"I know." I flick my eyes towards the hanging rope and feel my lunch resurfacing. Maybe the salmon was a bad idea.

"You should go join the others. I believe they are about to begin." Joshua eyes the soldiers walking the convict into the courtyard. Without saying a word, I move away from the men lining the walls and closer to the maids from within Castle Rae. My black hair sticks to my forehead as the morning sun pelts down from above.

The King and his daughter seem to be having a heated discussion and don't notice the commotion on the ground floor. People throw rotten food and stones at the tall man with the shaven head who strolls towards the wooden platform. He sneer's as he gazes at those around him. His shoulders rolled back as he walks up the stairs towards the hanging rope.

The Queen shushes the King and Princess as if reminding them where we are as she gestures out towards the crowd. The King gives his daughter an evil glare before getting to his feet to greet the awaiting hordes beneath him.

"Good men and women of Castle Rae, today we will witness the death of Duke Stephan's second in charge. The vile and aggressive Rod Fern. He planned and killed over thirty innocent men and women of the Sway as they refused to defer their loyalty away from me.

"Let this be known to all those wishing to do the same. We see you. And your crimes will not go unpunished. Executioner, he's all yours." The King's words are final as the courtyard breaks out into a thunderous roar.

People are applauding as the guards tie the rope around Rod's neck and even though I want to look away, I know I mustn't. The King would deem it as treason if I was not watching. He would see it as though I approved of their actions, and I don't want that. I just can't stand the sight of their necks breaking.

"Any last words?" The priest standing off to the side asks the prisoner in a low drawl. The crowd goes silent as they want to hear what he has to say. Rod takes a moment to peer out at those below him before raising his face to the King.

"The Duke wants what's rightfully his and is willing to do whatever it takes to get it. He is coming. That is all." Rod spits at the floor as a sickening grin appears across his lips. He slightly pulls on his restraints, and I see all the guards slightly move forward in my peripheral vision. They're all ready to strike at any given moment. Exactly how they are trained to be.

"Very well." The priest says and nods to the executioner. He steps forward and places a brown sack over the prisoner's head. He returns to the lever which will release the floor but stops. He glances over at the King who gives him a definite nod and in one quick pull, the floor gives way and there is a loud crack as Rod's neck breaks. Bile rises in my throat, but I swallow it down. I will not allow the King or Queen to see me in such a manner. I must be strong.

Everyone is silent as we watch the man's body slightly sway from side to side. A crow chirps high above as the King clears his throat. "That will be all everyone, you may leave." He booms and a second later everyone barrels for the exit. I see I'm not the only one who wants to be anywhere else but here.

I eye Joshua as I pass the gate and give him a little nod. He knows I will see him later as we always eat supper together.

I make my way down into the maid's quarters and can't seem to get Rod's words out of my head. Rod made it sound as if there was something else, other than the crown, that the Duke was after. But what could it be? There's no point deliberating over it now. He is gone and I must get back to work.

2

"Sadie, can you come in here please," The Queen calls from her sitting room. I place her laundry on the settee in the middle of her closet and return to her side. She is lying on her day bed with a book in one hand and the other arm covering her forehead. By the look on her face, she's not intrigued by the story at all.

"Yes ma'am?" I ask standing by her feet. Sophie, the Queen's other maid, is dusting the shelves. She turns her ears towards us; obviously curious as to why I was called and not her.

Queen Sarah huffs out a sigh, "Would you mind fetching my daughter? I need to speak with her." She asks, swinging her feet to the floor and placing the book on the table. A sickening feeling washes over me at the thought of having to retrieve that woman. One of the only bad things about working within the castle, is having to deal with her. The Queen's golden locks surround her face, making her look even more regal in the early afternoon sun.

“Yes, ma’am right away,” I curtsy and head for the door, grabbing the laundry basket on my way out. I do not doubt that Queen Sarah is going to confront the Princess about the show she and her father put on today. That was definitely not proper etiquette. As I pass through the open door, I hear the Queen speak again.

“Sophie, would you mind fetching us some tea, please? You know that horrible flavour my daughter likes, the one from Gosha. I can never remember the name of it. However, I’ll take camomile with honey. Thank you.”

“Right away, Your Majesty,” Sophie scurries out the door after me with the duster in hand. “It sucks to be you,” she giggles, as she matches my stride. We turn a corner and see three guards heading our way. None of them I recognise, so they must be new.

“Well thanks, I wish I was fetching the tea instead of her royal pain.”

“Good day ladies,” One of the cute guards tips his hat towards us as he passes by. Shocked by how handsome he is we both giggle our replies. Why do they always look so good in uniform?

“Well, I’m not switching if that’s what you’re asking. You are always better at getting her to move than I,” She says, tucking an orange strand of hair back underneath her bonnet. Cleaning the Queen’s room is definitely the most tiring job of all. I’m glad I wasn’t given that task to do today.

“Liar, and for a matter of fact, I was not asking, just stating the obvious,” I smile, as I wave goodbye and quickly duck into the laundry room. I place her Majesty's basket on the counter and head back out the door. Taking a deep breath, I make my way through the maze of hallways until I'm standing just outside Princess Hayley's chambers. From the sounds emitting from within the room, it appears she is throwing a tantrum. There are grunts followed by the sound of something breaking. Maybe I'll just wait a few minutes.

"What's going on with her?" I ask Kyle, the guard assigned to stand outside her door. He flinches at the sound of glass shattering behind him.

"Not sure, she's been like this since we came back from the hanging," he says, with a grim look on his face.

"Hmm, has anyone been in there since we came back?" I stare at his blackened out armour. Why the King chose black I have no idea. It's the hardest colour to keep clean.

"Not that I've seen." Kyle peers down the hallway as we hear footsteps approaching. It's just her Highness's lady's maids. They giggle and smile as they pass Kyle while they shove me out of the way to get to the door. Rachael has always been jealous that the Queen chose me instead of her.

"WHAT?!" The Princess yells from the other side of the door.

"It's just us Your Highness, may we come in?" Rachael asks as they stand there waiting for a reply. We hear footsteps approaching on the other side of the door before it unlocks and swings wide open. Her Highness steps to the side allowing them to enter and is about to shut the door when she gets a glimpse of me.

"What do you want?" She huffs as she crosses her arms over her chest. Her talon long fingernails grabbing hold of her biceps. I flick my eyes up to her face and see the natural make up she was wearing earlier has been replaced by something a little darker. Did she do that herself? She looks horrible.

Her long brown hair has come loose of its binds and trails in pieces down her back. Her purple sundress has what I can only presume is red wine spilt all down the front of it. And she is supposed to address the Queen looking like that? What a mess.

"Sorry for the intrusion your Highness, but the Queen requests your presence." I lower myself into a curtsy while trying not to screw up my nose. I take a step back and shift my eyes to the floor as I know how she hates it when people stare.

"Well, that's just great, what in the realm does she want?" The Princess exclaims, throwing her arms into the air.

"I'm not sure your Highness, she only said she would like to speak with you," I say softly, risking a glance at her face. Her brows have been shaped on the thicker side, making her look like she has two giant caterpillars resting on her face. The mole on her left cheek stands out even more against the darker tones of her make up. I wonder why she would wear such atrocious colours. It's completely unnatural.

“Ah, fine!” She huffs and storms off down the hallway with Kyle in tow. I feel sorry for him having to endure her on a daily basis.

Before I leave, I peer into her chambers. There is glass and ceramic shattered everywhere. Rachael and Molly are gazing at the floor, trying to decide where to start. All I know is they better be quick because her Highness would probably chuck another fit if she were to come back to the room looking like this.

Knowing my place, I quickly dash after the two people heading towards the Queen's chambers. Thankfully when the Queen is angry, she just sits in silence. I’ve only ever had to clean up broken glass when it was an accident, and that was many years ago.

I round the next corner and witness her Highness forgoing formalities as she barges into the Queen's sitting room.

“How dare you? This is not your chamber! Leave and enter properly girl, where are your manners?” The Queen yells at her daughter. I know the Princess is taking extra etiquette classes now more than ever, but I fear her manners are only getting worse.

“Argh, first you call me in here and now you’re asking me to leave?” Princess Hayley calls out like she’s on the verge of tears. What happened before between her and the King?

“Stop acting like such a child girl, you are the future Queen of Castle Rae. I only asked you to get up, walk out the door and wait until you’re properly introduced before you may enter." I move closer to the door as the Princess storms out, turns around and waits. She flicks her eyes at me and gives me a dreadful glare. What did I do?

"Sadie, are you out there?" I startle at the Queen's voice and rush through the open door. I hear Hayley's frustrated sigh behind me yet ignore it. I'm doing my duty after all.

"Your Majesty?" I utter politely as I curtsey in front of her. She has a look of pure joy on her face when I step foot into the room, however it quickly fades to sadness when she opens her mouth to speak.

"Thank you for retrieving my daughter, would you please see her in?" She sits on the same day bed as before. She's had Sophie correct her golden locks, which seems to make her beautiful yellow sun dress shine against her radiant skin. Thankfully after the hanging, she changed out of her black mourning dress. I will never understand why someone who agrees with the hanging would insist on wearing black. I'm also amazed the King has never said anything about it.

"Yes ma'am." I curtsey and turn towards her Highness, "She will see you now." The Princess smooths out the front of her dress as she gives me yet another death stare while passing through the open door. I ignore it and close the door behind her.

"Sadie?" The Queen calls.

"Yes ma'am," I fold my hands in front of me and straighten my back. The Queen gives me one of her small smiles as she reaches for her cup of tea.

"You and Sophie may tend to your other duties. Kyle will send word once we are done." She takes a sip of her tea and turns her stare towards her daughter sitting opposite her.

"Yes, Your Majesty." I curtsey and quickly exit the room. Princess Hayley has been extra tiring lately and I think the Queen has finally had enough. I really didn't want to be around anyway to witness the conversation likely to happen.

"Good luck," I whisper to Kyle as I pass by and scurry off down the hall.

It's just after midday so that means that Joshua would probably be patrolling the gardens right about now. Maybe if luck were on our side, we could sneak off for a quick minute alone. If only we were so lucky. Every time we've tried that in the past, someone always catches us. Not that it's a crime, just not something that should be done during the daytime.

3

"Good day my lady, what brings you around these parts?" Joshua tips his hat forward, as he glances around to see if anyone is there before placing a kiss on my cheek. The notion brings a smile to my face. He may be tall, but he is still able to hide perfectly behind an apple tree in the middle of the Queen's gardens. All the flowers around us are in full bloom, creating such a sweet aroma.

"Her Majesty is having a conversation with the Princess, and as I'm up to date with my duties, I have some free time. How about you? Can you spare a moment?" I ask eagerly, wanting to escape with him to the shadows. It has been a tiring day and I want nothing more than to wrap my arms around him and kiss him feverishly.

His eyes light up with excitement until he peers over my shoulder and then his face falls. I glance back and see his Majesty the King walking around a rosemary bush with his advisers in tow. They are heading towards the armoury in the outer regions of the castle. The King only goes down there in times of war. Has the Duke finally declared battle after his brother killed his second in charge?

"Sorry, but it looks like I won't be able to escape today. I do however have something I want to show you later tonight, during supper. I found them while helping the groundsmen clean out a storeroom after the hanging." There is movement on my left and we both swing our stare to see more guards heading down towards the armoury. What's going on?

I peer up at Joshua alarmed, as he leans forward and kisses my cheek once more. "Don't be afraid my love, but I have to go. I'll see you later on," he whispers into my ear before adjusting his hat and walking off to join another officer patrolling the gardens.

They walk for a few metres side by side, exchanging small talk before stopping at the steps that lead down to the fountains. They are staring down at the armoury. Intrigued by what's going on, I fold my hands in front of me and quickly walk over to see what's got their attention.

The armoury being roughly the same size as the stables beside it, is surrounded by at least fifty soldiers, all gearing up. They're covering themselves with metal plated armour, and some are gathering bows and quivers, while others are arming themselves with battle axes.

"Joshua?" I question quietly. I may not know the other guard standing beside my love, but I do not wish for him to hear me. He did not witness the kiss Joshua placed on my cheek earlier and I want to keep it that way. I'm standing less than three feet away and by the slight movement of Joshua's head, I know he heard me.

"Excuse me, ma'am," Joshua fills his voice with authority, like the one he generally uses when he's ready to lead an army. Knowing I mustn't disobey a Knight, I turn to face him, "Yes, Sir?" I say softly.

"I think it would be best that you go back inside. I'm not too sure what all the commotion is about however, I feel there is something or someone within the castle who requires your attention more." I know he's not meaning to be rude; he just wants to get me out of here. He doesn't know what's going on himself and thinks it's best that I'm not in the way if something is to eventuate.

"Yes, Sir," I duck my head and head towards the doors leading back into the castle. I'm passing the rosemary bush when I glance back and see him staring over his shoulder at me. I produce a small wave and a smile as I step over the threshold and see Kyle heading my way.

"She's ready for you now," he utters tiredly. I see the bags hanging under his eyes and make a mental note to mention it to Joshua. Knowing he would be able to organise to cut Kyle a break and get him away from her Highness for at least a day or two. I wonder who Kyle would have had to have pissed off to be given the job of looking after her.

"Thank you," Kyle stops mid stride and waits until I've caught up before turning around. "How was it?" I ask hesitantly. By the look on his face, it didn't go too well.

"Well, it started quiet, that was until the Queen said something about the Princess looking like a tramp. That was when I heard the first item shatter." I shiver at the thought of having to clean up broken glass. I hope she didn't trash the place. "Did you know, I've never heard the Queen raise her voice before? Not once in the thirteen years, I've been working here. That daughter of hers really brings out her angry side. The Princess acts like a child, not someone who can rule over our sovereign nation."

"I couldn't agree more, but Kyle you must remember to be careful. Your thoughts may be the death of you. The King's men would see it as treason to be talking so poorly of our future Queen. Especially so openly and with the Duke breathing down the King's neck." I look down the passageways as we pass by and thankfully there is no one in sight. Everyone would probably be in the dining hall preparing for supper right about now.

"Sorry, you're right." We round the next corner and her Majesty's chamber's come into view. Light filters out through the open door as I hear Sophie sweeping the floor inside. Shards of glass clink together as they move along the hard wooden floor. We stop directly outside the door and I'm afraid to peer inside. Who knows what mess lies beyond the threshold?

"It's alright to speak your mind, Kyle, just remember to be careful. Not everyone has the same views as you... Anyway, I best be off, I need to help Sophie clean up before supper." I give him a grateful smile and wave goodbye as I turn and step foot into the Queen's sitting room. Oh my...

The daybed is overturned, as well as the table in the middle of the room. Books lie scattered all over the room and glass shards line the floor. Who knew that the Princess could make such a mess in such a short amount of time?

"Are you going to just stand there, or have you forgotten that the Queen is having tea with the priest right before supper?" Sophie looks frazzled and I don't blame her. We have until mid-afternoon to get this room looking somewhat proper before the priest arrives. This meeting has been in motion for months and we cannot allow a ruined room to get in the way of that.

"Sorry, I'll go grab another broomstick," I mutter quickly before dashing back out of the room to fetch one from the cupboard. Hopefully, we will be able to get it straightened up in time.

4

"Father you must understand, my daughter must be protected. She is in grave danger, especially if Duke Stephan's men make it inside these walls." Queen Sarah stares down at the priest sitting on her daybed. He gazes at her like he simply does not care and it's really starting to annoy me. How could he be so thoughtless with the Queens wishes? Does he not realise that she could potentially end his clerical position if she chooses to? She is being generous in letting him remain in power, definitely going by the show he's putting on today.

"Your Majesty, I completely understand your worries however, I know for certain that your husband has it under control, so there is no need for the church to intervene.

The Princess will stay here, where her people need her. When she turns eighteen in a couple of months it will be up to her how we will deal with her safety, but until then, it's up to the King.

My apologies your Majesty but, our time is now up. People need my attention in the confessional, and I must not make them wait. I bid you a good day your Majesty." At least the slime ball bows his head before rushing out the door. He didn't even have the nerve to wait for the Queen's response. She's glaring in his wake, and I know she is about to explode.

His Holiness's only response to her concerns was that the King will handle it. Which he will, but he can't always be around to protect his daughter. Kyle is by her side from sun-up to sun-down, but he may not be enough. I wonder what the Queen knows that has her as worried as she is.

Maybe it's because if the Princess dies, there is no other heir to take the throne. Queen Sarah tried many times but was never able to conceive another child. I remember witnessing all the tears and heartaches while growing up. My mother never shielded me from any of it. She wanted me to see what was going on in the world so I would know how to handle the situation when it was my time to serve.

If King Roger also dies, the throne will inevitably fall to Duke Stephan. He will finally get his wish of being King of Castle Rae and would have plenty of time to produce an heir; as he is much younger than King Roger. Somehow though, it feels that it's more than that, but I just can't think what it might be.

The Queen turns towards Sophie who is standing off to the side of the room. "Sophie, can you please fetch Sir Joshua. I believe at this hour he would be helping the guards down in the courtyard." We have been here all afternoon and I'm very much in need of a break. It has been mentally draining listening to the Queen and his Holiness banter for hours on end.

"Right away, Your Majesty." Sophie quickly curtseys and walks out the door. The Queen looks up at the portrait above her mantel and sighs.

"If only times were as easy as they were back then." Within a large golden frame is a painting of the royals that was commissioned five years ago for the Queen's fortieth birthday. With her daughter sitting proudly on her lap, the Queen looks radiant as her smile stares back at us.

"They may be again Your Majesty," I say cleaning up the teacups from the centre table. It is almost time to recede to the dining hall for supper and with the way my stomach is growling, I hope the cooks have prepared a mighty feast.

"I'm afraid that will never happen, not with the way Stephan is proceeding. If only Roger would cooperate." Queen Sarah stares deep into the mantel and I almost beg her to say more but there's a knock at the door. "Come in," she says as she smooths out the front of her golden gown and folds her hands in front of her.

"You asked to see me, Your Majesty?" Joshua bows before his Queen, but I don't miss his sneaky glance towards me before he does. It has been hard for us lately to find time alone, especially with Stephans men breaking through the gates. Every time we think we finally have a moment's peace; he gets pulled away to fight the onslaught of troops heading our way. Hopefully, tonight will be different.

"Yes, I did and thank you for coming so soon. I would like to allocate more soldiers to protect my daughter." The Queen raises her chin, showing her authority. She will not back down on this matter no matter who stands in her way. If the church won't help her and neither will her husband, the King, her next best option is to go to the man who will lead the charge. My man, the castellan of Castle Rae.

"But Kyle..." Joshua begins but the Queen cuts him off.

"Is doing a wonderful job, but I want more. I need at least two or three to be able to put my worries at ease."

"But Your Majesty, the King will not allow me to move..." Joshua scratches his head and then rakes his fingers through his unruly brown hair. Queen Sarah is giving him an almighty stare and I know he is about to give in. He knows what the King will say if he moves the troops, but he is not able to deny the Queen her wishes. "... I'll have to relocate some of the men, but I may be able to get you two more Your Majesty. Only two though, no more." He lifts his chin too, standing his ground. I smirk as I watch their stand-off. It would be kind of cute if we weren't discussing such dire circumstances.

"That sounds perfect, thank you, Sir Joshua. If King Roger has any issues about it, tell him to come see me." She gets to her feet and walks over to stand in front of him. She looks like the sun in her beautiful dress, while he looks like death in his blackened out armour. You can see the trust and admiration passing between, it is impossible to miss.

"I will, your Majesty." He nods his head in acknowledgment as he peers down at his Queen. A small smile plays on his lips, and I begin to wonder what it's about.

"Thank you again, you may leave."

"Good evening, Your Majesty." He bows before seeing himself out. At least one good thing came out of today.

5

The dining hall is filled to the brim with patrons, who yell and speak so loudly it's making my ears ring. I sit down at my normal spot and start digging into my meal. I'm absolutely famished. Once Princess Hayley left the Queen's sitting room, we were left with such a mess that we had to work our way through lunch.

"Did you know the King is going to kick my arse for moving the troops," Joshua says with his head slightly facing me. He has a rather large turkey leg in hand but chuckles as I shove a huge spoonful of potatoes into my mouth. It's very un-lady like, I know, but at this moment I really don't care. I swallow my food and smile at him.

"Sorry... But you heard the Queen, if the King has an issue with it, tell him to take it up with her."

"True, but that's easier said than done. You know how he hates it when people interfere. Especially if it's his darling

Queen." I had almost forgotten about the time when Queen Sarah stopped a flogging.

Many years ago, a soldier was caught trying to switch sides and that is punishable by death. However, this time, King Roger wanted to make an example out of the man, to show the full force of what may happen to anyone else who tried to leave.

The poor soldier received sixty-three lashings before Queen Sarah stormed in and called an end to it. His back was torn to shreds and his wounds were cut so deep, there was no hope of survival. The King was proving his dominance that day and the Queen wouldn't stand for it.

"Hopefully, everything will be alright. You mentioned earlier to her Majesty that Kyle will suffice as her guard. Have you not noticed how tired he is lately? He is exhausted and in need of a break. I hope it's alright for me to say that he gets one when the new guards arrive." Joshua gives me a bewildered look but then slightly nods his head. For a moment there I thought he was going to object.

Joshua understands how tiring it can be to watch her Highness. That was one of his first assignments as a soldier until he got called to the front line. There he fought with all his might and bravery and came home a Knight. I will never forget the look on his face when the King announced their victory. We finally won a battle against the Highlands. That hadn't been achieved since before I was born.

"Alright he will rest, but we needn't talk about it anymore." There is laughter on my left and I turn to see

Sophie smiling at her partner Greggory. He gazes upon her with so much love and I wish Joshua and I could be so open and do the same. He is a Knight, and I am just a lady's maid. I am afraid our people would frown upon him for being with such a lower class.

On the other hand, I don't think Joshua would care. He has told me many times how much he loves me and how he can't wait until I'm eighteen. Then I'll have the choice of whether to leave or stay at the castle. If we leave, we can be wed and spend the rest of our days free in the country. If we stay, we will conform to the normality of Castle Rae and probably spend the rest of our lives in secret, for I do not wish people to judge me or him for who we love.

I turn back to my love and notice he is digging deep into the pocket of his cloak. I draw my eyebrows together as Joshua produces a handful of folded up pieces of parchment. Without letting anyone else see them, he passes them to me underneath the table.

"Here take these, hide them in your apron." He says quietly as he glances around before stopping to stare directly into my eyes. My heart skips a beat at his expression as I reach for the parchment. They feel coarse and weathered against my fingers, hinting at the fact they may be many years old.

"What are they?" I ask shoving them into the front of my apron. Joshua leans forward and pretends to grab something off the floor behind me. His mouth is so close to my ear that my breath hitches in my throat.

"They are letters. Written by... I don't know who, but they are all addressed to none other than the Duke of Castle Rae." He whispers so quietly into my ear that I almost thought I misheard him. Can it be? The Duke hasn't lived in Castle Rae for as long as I've been alive. He and the King had some sort of falling out and he banished his younger brother to live in the Highlands. I heard stories about that day, King Roger gave his brother a very public ultimatum, die via hanging or banishment. It was the only time King Roger showed any mercy.

"Where did you find them?" I ask quietly as Joshua rights himself and pretends to continue with his meal.

"In a storage room in the west wing. They were inside an old satchel hidden in a wooden chest. If the box didn't break open when we were moving it, I would never have discovered them. I saw the name Stephan Tailgate scribbled on top and knew that they were of importance. Before anyone noticed though I quickly hid them inside my cloak." Joshua takes a huge bite out of his turkey leg and raises his goblet to a soldier passing by. He tries to act as casual as he can while he turns his ears slightly towards me.

"Did you read them?" I whisper looking around to see if anyone has noticed us conversing way more than usual. Thankfully though everyone seems too preoccupied with their meals to notice.

"Yes. There is a secret message written within those pages, but I just can't figure out what. You have to read them Sadie. We will discuss this more when you have." He glances discretely towards me, and I nod my head. I understand that this conversation must end. We have probably brought too much attention to ourselves already. If there really is a secret here though, I will find it.

"What are you two love birds whispering about?" My gaze shoots over Joshua's shoulder to the man standing behind him dressed in blackened out armour. His smile is broad however his eyes are dark, the eyes of a man who has seen many horrors on the battlefields.

"Oh, you know, the usual. Just how I want to whisk her away, get married by fire light and make her have all my babies." Joshua says casually, ending with a smile as Lance takes his seat on the other side of him. He looks over at me and I fake a nervous smile. Ducking my head, I turn my eyes back to my food and try to make it look like Joshua and I were not deep in conversation. Lance sees us talk all the time but never so hush hush. I wonder what Joshua will say to get us out of this one.

"You know you can scream for help anytime you want Sadie, I'll always be around to get this great big lug away from you." Lance gives me a wink before sinking his teeth into his own enormous turkey leg. Where in the realm did they find such humongous turkeys?

"Me?" Joshua asks horrified as he places his hand on his chest. He flicks his gaze between the two of us before stopping to look at me. "It's more like I would have to get him away from you."

"Come on man, you know I would make a much better suiter for her. I've had many more lovers than you." Lance gives me another wink, but this time bile rises in my throat. He may be an attractive man, but his reputation precedes him.

Lance has had many courtiers, a fact that's not possible to debate. Women love to make it publicly known when they have slept with the devilish Knight of Castle Rae. They make it sound like they have won a medal or something. They just don't realise how it makes them look in the eyes of others. Lance has even made the mistake a few times of sleeping with the enemy, although those mistakes have always gained us vital intel.

"And that makes you the better companion?" Joshua looks at him sceptically.

"Absolutely," He winks at me over Joshua's shoulder, and I duck my head as I fake yet another nervous smile. I turn my eyes to the opposite side of the room and see that the Queen is staring at me. She has a blank expression on her face, and I get this weird feeling that I may have done something wrong.

I'm about to rise from my seat when I see her slightly shake her head. Her eyes are pleading with me to stay put as she replaces her blank expression with a smile and returns to conversing with her daughter.

She has been acting out of sorts lately and I'm beginning to worry. About a month ago, King Roger rounded up more able men from the Sway to help keep his brother out. It was around that time that the Queen started acting strange. As the King started stationing more troops around the yard, the Queen picked up more tasks of her own and filled her days with meetings and luncheons with important people.

A lot of the time they only discuss politics and how her daughter would be treated during her reign. However, it's the moments when Sophie and I aren't there that I believe she discusses the real reason for calling the meetings. I only wish I knew what's on her mind.

I finish off my meal while I watch the Queen from a far. She smiles and laughs at something someone said, appearing utterly carefree. Princess Hayley on the other hand looks as if she has swallowed something sour. Her face is contorted into a weird expression, and I can't help but laugh.

Joshua's fingers brush against my leg and for a complete moment, I forgot he was there. My breath hitches in my throat as I feel his fingers run up and down my leg in a circular motion.

He loudly clears his throat "I believe it's time for me to retire, the King put me on dawn duty again." He huffs out his annoyance while Lance smiles with glee.

"Sucks to be you. I'm going to find me a lass to bed as I don't need to report until dusk." Lance leans back in his chair as his eyes shift about the room.

"How did you manage to pull that?" Joshua eyes him inquisitively.

"I'm the King's favourite," Lance declares while smiling as he gets to his feet. "I think I see a beautiful golden lass just over there so nighty night folks, I'll see you tomorrow."

"Good night," I whisper as Lance strolls behind me heading towards the new lady's maid that arrived from the Sway. Sandy has been here almost a week and with the way all the men are staring at her, she's lucky she has survived this long without Lance stealing her away.

"My chamber, now," Joshua demands quietly. His dark eyes meet mine as he gets to his feet before he turns and heads for the door. I look over at the Queen and see she has yet to finish her meal, so I know I have a little time to myself.

To avoid being too obvious, I wait a few more minutes before I rise to my feet, brush the breadcrumbs from my apron and head out of the hall. Once I'm free of prying eyes I dash down the hallway to my lover's chamber. The door is open, so I forgo a knock and barge on in. The door slams shut behind me and I startle, jumping almost a full foot into the air. I whirl around and see Joshua staring down at me with a heated stare. Without another word, I rush forward and wrap my arms around his neck pulling his face down to meet mine.

Joshua grabs hold of my butt and lifts me so high that I wrap my legs around his waist. Without breaking the kiss, he walks us over and sits down on the edge of his cot. He's removed his armour and only his padded shirt remains. His lips are fast and eager as he uses his tongue to open my mouth. A little moan escapes my lips and I feel him groan beneath me. I've longed for this moment all day. The one time when I can truly be myself around him.

"If you're going to start making little noises like that, I won't be able to hold back." He says pulling his face away from mine. He sweeps my long black hair over my shoulder and starts trailing kisses down the side of my neck.

"Sorry, it just slipped out," I giggle breathlessly. His lips feel like ice against my overly heated skin. "Just three more months, then we can finally be together." Once I'm eighteen we will finally be able to wed and leave the confines of this castle. I know the Queen will be saddened to see me leave but it's my choice. I have longed for this day since the moment my mother passed away three years ago. She always dreamed of the country and yet she never left. She believed her duty to the crown was more important than her happiness.

"I cannot wait to have you, my love." He pulls me forward and I feel him growing beneath me. His longing and his yearning for the love we are yet to fully experience.

We have been together for almost two years and not once has Joshua ever tried to force himself upon me. He understands my wishes to be married before sex, it was the one thing I promised my mother I would do.

Joshua moves his head a little bit lower and begins placing tiny little kisses along my collarbone before moving back up towards my mouth. He tastes sweet, like fine wine as he massages his tongue against mine. His fingers work their way into my hair and for a few minutes, I am lost in the feel of him. If only we could stay like this.

I pull my lips away and rest my forehead against his, "I'm sorry my love, but I have to go."

"I know, her Majesty would most certainly be finished by now." Joshua leans back and places a gentle kiss on my forehead. I wish I didn't have to go but I know if I don't leave now, the Queen will begin to wonder where I am.

"Until tomorrow," I whisper giving him one final kiss as I climb off his lap.

"Until tomorrow," He replies as he stares at me with total love and affection. I open the door slightly and peak my head out. The coast is clear. Turning back, I give him a little wave and dash out of the room.

As quickly as I can, I rush up to the Queen's chambers and notice that I'm the first one to return. Thank goodness, and it gives me time to prepare her Majesty's room in readiness for her to retire.

6

"That will be all ladies, you may go," Queen Sarah announces from her bed with a book in hand. She looks so serene while entranced by the pages of a new romance story by a local writer. She was saddened by something when she came back from the dining hall, and it killed Sophie and me not to ask why. The Queen usually shares all her feelings with us but as of late, she is keeping more to herself. There is something she doesn't want us to know.

"Have a good evening Your Majesty," Sophie and I say in unison as we curtsey and head out the door. I am so ready for bed. It has been such a tiring day, especially with the hanging and everything else that's been happening today. I wonder how Duke Stephan will react now. King Roger really poked the bear this time.

"I wonder what made her Majesty so upset, did something happen at supper? I was too busy with Greggory to notice anything else." Sophie says sheepishly as we head down the hallway leading towards the laundry room. The

Queen's blank expression in the dining hall crosses my mind but I decide to keep it to myself and say nothing. I don't want to worry Sophie over what may be nothing.

"Not to my knowledge." We enter the laundry room and I place the Queen's basket on the counter. The room is eerily quiet at this hour as the cleaners are on break until lights out.

I am glad I don't have their job, I wouldn't be able to stay awake after the lights go out. I know that they have candlelight to see by, but I prefer to sleep when it's dark. "Tomorrow, would you like to collect the Queen's breakfast, as I know Greggory will probably be rotating in the hall, or would you like to collect the laundry?" I ask, making sure that the Queen's clothes from earlier are all pressed and ready to be put away tomorrow.

"Is that really a question?" Sophie places her hands behind her back and rocks back and forth on her heels. The smile she has for her beau lights up the entire room and I can't help but smile back.

"Silly me, I should have known." I shake my head as we enter the hallway and walk back the way we came. We veer off towards the maid's quarters and my heartbeat picks up as we near the corridor leading down towards Joshua's room. I have seen him a few times before, lurking in the corridor at this hour but tonight is not one of them.

"When are you going to find yourself a man Sadie? I have seen the way the soldiers look at you and one of them is bound to have grabbed your attention by now." She peers over at me like a big sister and I can't help the blush that creeps over my skin. If only she knew...

"I have seen them, it's just... I'm waiting for the right one." I utter shrugging my shoulders.

"You can't wait forever," Sophie is only five years older than me but sometimes it feels like more. "Anyway, I'll see you at dawn," she gives me a small wave as she breaks off and heads down a corridor to the left. I round the next corner and enter my chambers, shutting the door behind me.

"Finally," I whisper and head over to the candle stick. I light a match and the room comes to life as I begin to strip off my clothes. I hear the sound of crumpled parchment and my heart stops for a moment, I completely forgot about the letters I had hidden in the front of my apron.

Dashing over to the fire light I hold one up and read the words scribbled on the front

Sir Stephan Tailgate

"No way, Joshua was right," I place the parchment on the counter and quickly dash to the corner to bathe. Swiftly, I throw on my nightdress before returning to open the letters. Grabbing the first one off the stack, I carefully peel back the pages. The parchment is so old that it almost crumbles beneath my fingers. I hold it up to the light and begin to read...

My Dearest Stephan

It has been weeks since you left. My nights are cold and lonely without you here. I miss you, my love. Your father announced today that he will be renouncing his title by the end of the week, making your brother, King. You must come home before he does. We need you here, I need you here. Who knows what your brother will do once he gains so much power? Your mother and I beg of you to return my love, please resolve the matter with the Sway quickly and come home.

We need you, desperately.

Yours always

Z

But the Duke never came home, not permanently anyway. Upon arrival, the King and his brother had a very public disagreement and the Duke was banished from that day forth. Or so I've been told. Knowing the King as I do, I can understand why this person was so afraid for him to reign.

Without another thought, I pick up the next one and start reading...

My Dearest Stephan

Where are you? Your mother told me that she too has sent word, and yet no one knows where you are. We are worried about you, my love. Your brother's coronation is tomorrow, and we were hoping you'd be back in time to stop it. Back in time to request the duel that we all know you'd win. You are kinder, stronger and braver than he and that is why you'd make a much better King than your brother, all of Castle Rae knows that.

Just come home, my love.

Yours always

Z

Stephan, a better King? I was under the impression that he was even more of a tyrant than his brother. But according to these letters, he's not. In saying that though, I have never met the man, nor will I probably ever. And yet, this person and the previous Queen both thought that Stephan would make a better ruler than Roger. So, what happened? Why was he banished?

"LIGHT'S OUT!" The hall guard shouts from down the corridor and I know I have only a short amount of time left before they check to see who is still up. I refold the parchment and place it upon the dresser before blowing out the candle.

Maybe it's about time I start asking what really started this war between the brothers. Only then might I learn the truth behind what's hidden on these pages.

7

"Good morning your Majesty," I say as I awkwardly curtsy with the Queen's laundry basket under one arm and the new shoes that arrived from Bodega under the other. Her eyes light up with excitement as she glances at the box. I walk into her closet to drop the laundry basket on the floor before returning to give her her new shoes. I remember the Queen telling me about these when she returned from Bodega almost a year ago. A woman of the court was wearing a pair of these beautifully handcrafted shoes and Queen Sarah fell in love with them.

I place the box on the table and I barely have time to remove my hands before the Queen flips off the lid.

"I can't believe they are finally here," she reaches into the rectangular shaped box and produces the most magnificent pair of shoes I have ever seen.

The fabric is a glorious shade of gold that has gems along the top that gleam in the sunlight. They create tiny little stars that bounce off the walls. "Aren't they to die for? The ones the woman wore in court were silver however, I thought they would look much better in gold, and I was right." Queen Sarah's smile is infectious, and I can't help but smile with her.

"They are splendid Your Majesty," I utter as I curtsey and excuse myself from the room. I would love to stand there all day watching her beam over her new shoes, but I have work to do. This laundry will not put itself away.

My morning is filled with endless chores and before I know it, the sun is at its highest peak.

"Ladies you may leave to have your meals. Also, I won't be needing you for some time, so there's no need to rush back. I believe I'm going to have a quiet afternoon reading, as long as no one interrupts me." Queen Sarah announces from her day bed. She glances our way for only a moment before pondering over her book once more. That scandalous romance story really has her intrigued.

"Yes, Your Majesty," Sophie and I gather up the sheets from the Queens floor and head out into the hallway. It's becoming more regular for the Queen to let us have longer breaks. I have found the older she gets, the more she wants to be alone.

"Sadie?" Sophie says next to me. Her red hair shines in the midday sun as we pass by an open window. There is chatter down in the courtyard and it's so loud that I'm intrigued to find out what all the fuss is about.

"Yes," I reply, while I glance out another window to see if I can see anything.

"I'm leaving." She says bluntly and I stop dead in my tracks. I knew this was coming. The moment she wed Greggory I knew she was going to leave Castle Rae. She always spoke about obtaining a farm dew east, out past Fairwind Forest. Her passion has always been to raise a family away from the confines of this castle. I'm so proud of her for finally following her dreams.

"When?" I ask not leaving myself any room to try and convince her to stay. I am happy she is following her dreams, I'm just worried about who will replace her.

"In five days' time. I've already spoken with her Majesty. I will be replaced by a much younger maid from the Sway, and I need to train her over the coming days to take my place."

"I'm so happy for you Sophie, truly. I wish you luck in your endeavours although, I am really going to miss you." I would hug her if it weren't for the pile of laundry I have bundled up in my arms.

"And I, you. You've become so dear to me but it's time for me to move on and start a family. Greggory has also resigned and has already gone forth, making preparations to the land where we are going to make our new home. I'm so excited Sadie, this is what I've longed for, for a very long time."

"I know and I wish you both the best. Maybe once I find my special someone, I can come and visit you." I utter hopefully. I yearn for the day that I too can leave this place, but it won't be anytime soon. Joshua is needed here, and we both know it. No one is a greater leader than him.

"Absolutely, you're welcome anytime," Sophie says fondly as we gaze at each other. My heart beams with joy to see her so happy. "I have to go meet my replacement, so I'll meet up with you soon." She says, already backing away.

I nod my head, "I'll see you later," and turn to walk down towards the laundry room.

Inside the room, everyone is moving at a drastic pace as they try to get things either washed or dried. I've never seen so many people working at the same time, I wonder what all the fuss is about.

I'm about to ask what's going on when there is a tap on my shoulder, startling me from my thoughts. I turn quickly to see two of the King's personal guards clad in black and gold armour. My heart skips a beat at the sight of them.

"The King requests your presence. Now!" The one with blonde hair announces and my anxiety spikes. Oh no, what have I done? Not once in my entire life has the King ever requested to see me.

As quickly as I can, I nod my head and the guards turn on their heels, walking back out the door. Knowing what's good for me, I follow them. We walk through the labyrinth of hallways until we reach the King's own private chambers. Dread sits in the base of my stomach as the guards open the door and I see King Roger lounging in his day bed. One of the guards enters the room to announce my arrival and the King waves me in. With unsteady footing, I enter over the threshold and jump slightly as the door closes shut behind me.

"You requested to see me, Your Majesty," I say with a shaky breath.

"My wife, had a meeting with the high priest yesterday, why?" Knowing that I can't lie, I decide to tell the truth. Straightening my back, I try to show that I know exactly what I'm doing and really hope the Queen won't punish me for this.

"She requested that the church protect Princess Hayley," I say with as much courage in my voice as I can muster. Knowing that my fingers are shaking, I move my hands behind my back and knot them together.

"And why would she need protecting?" King Roger spits almost angrily as he sits up straighter in his chair. I get the feeling that I should watch what I say from here on out. His beady eyes roam down my body and I have to swallow the bile that rises in my throat. He is known to force himself upon women, and I dread the thought of him making me his target.

He raises his eyes to mine as a sickening smirk appears on his lips. Oh gosh, please no...

“I’m not too sure your Majesty, but I believe the Queen is just worried for her safety.”

“Really,” he says snidely, relaxing back in his chair. For a man in his fifties, he is quite good looking. Tall with grey hair and a muscular stature. If it weren’t for his darker side, I believe he would have women swooning at his feet instead of running away.

The King is known to be vile and mean, even more so behind closed doors. Especially with the women he beds. Not the kind of man I would like to be well acquainted with. “And what did Father John say?” He says almost smiling, as if he knows full well that the priest turned her down.

“He told the Queen that you have it under control,” I say truthfully. He gazes upon me with lust in his eyes and I beg the heavens to take me away from this place, away from this man, right now!

The angels know that I cannot deny the King if he wishes to have me. The last woman who tried ended up being hung for treason. Her last words told us so... This is all because I wouldn’t bed you... Her screams ring out in my memory as the King gets to his feet and starts slowly prowling towards me.

“And how did she take the news?” He mutters circling behind me. I feel his eyes roaming my body and I can’t calm my raging heart that's beating within my chest.

“Not good your Majesty.” He steps closer and I feel his body directly behind me. I want to scream for help but know that no one will come to my aid for fear of severe reprimand.

I close my eyes and prey that he does not advance. His fingertips sweep my hair over my shoulder, draping it down my back.

He moves his mouth next to my ear and whispers, "I'm glad," before placing a gentle kiss into the crook of my neck. I have to stop the tear that longs to escape as he moves his mouth back towards my ear. "Is there anything else you need to tell me?" His voice is threatening as the Queen's conversation with Joshua enters my mind.

"No, your Majesty, that is all." I declare with a slight shake of my breath. I really hope he doesn't notice how nervous he makes me feel, and not in a good way.

"Good." His fingers play with the hair draped over my shoulder and as quick as lightning, he grips me around the throat and pulls me flush against him. I'm gasping for air as his hot breath speaks into my ear. "If for whatever reason you've been lying to me Sadie Jaymes, I'm going to come after you, and you don't want to know the things I'll do." I pull at his hands begging for him to let go, but he only tightens his grip more.

He licks the side of my face before whirling us around and shoves me towards the closed door. "Now, get out!" The King shouts and the guards swiftly open the doors. I forgo formalities as I rush out of the room and run as fast as I can towards my own chambers.

People stare at me as I pass them in the hallway, but I don't care. I will not allow them to see the tears streaming down my face.

I finally make it to my chamber and slam the door shut once I'm inside. I barrel over to my cot and pick up my pillow, shoving it against my face. I scream with all the panic built up within me. I am in shock and shaking all over from what just happened!

My door swings open wide and in a flash, big strong arms circle around me and pick me up off the bed. Oh no, not again! I fight and scream for whoever it is to let me go but then a familiar scent hits my nose. I instantly stop. Joshua! Without a word, he sits down on the edge of the bed, resting me upon his lap. He holds me so gently while I weep into his chest.

"Lance told me the King had summoned you, but by the time I made it up to his chamber, you were already gone." His voice is soft against my ears. It feels like he's miles away although I know he is right beside me. "What happened my love," He asks cautiously.

"He... He..." I begin to stutter before swallowing passed the lump that's formed in my throat. "He kissed my neck and laid his hands around my throat. He tried to choke me. I.... He... He threatened to do worse if I were caught lying to him." I feel Joshua's anger rise as his body goes stiff. His breathing becomes heavy as he tries to hold himself back.

"I'm gonna kill him," Joshua seethes through gritted teeth, and yet fear like I've never felt before washes over me.

"Joshua you mustn't! I didn't lie to him. I just didn't tell him about your conversation with the Queen." I whisper hoarsely as my throat has become dry from all the screaming and crying. Panic rises within me even more once I lift my head and catch a glimpse of the death of our King, lingering in Joshua's stunning grey eyes.

"Tell me exactly what he wanted to know?" He asks through gritted teeth as he peers down at my neck. He sweeps my messy black hair over my shoulder trying to see if his Majesty left any marks.

"He wanted to know why the Queen requested a meeting with Father John," I mutter quietly. By the look in Joshua's eyes, there is most certainly a mark around my neck. His gaze turns deadly, and I feel his body shift beneath me.

"And you told him?" He asks sternly and a little too loudly and I shrink further within myself. Not once in all our time together have I ever seen Joshua so angry. I hear his teeth grinding together and know that his love for me is the only thing stopping him from going after the King this very instance. I think he realises I have endured enough male testosterone and violence for today.

"Of course I did, what else was I supposed to do?" I whisper quietly while lowering my head and resting it against his chest. His heartbeat is a steady rhythm, the complete opposite of mine.

"And?" His voice is lower than the last time but still loud enough that a passer-by would know that I have a man in my room. That's the last thing I need the maids whispering about.

"And nothing, he heard what he wanted to hear and threatened me with violence if I were caught lying, which I didn't." I raise my head again and gaze into his angry but concerned eyes. I plead with him to drop it.

There is nothing he can do to change what happened and even if he tried, the King would surely kill him for it. We stare at each other for what feels like an eternity before Joshua closes his eyes and rests his forehead against mine.

"I'm sorry Sadie, when I heard the King was looking for you, I was terrified. I knew his request wouldn't amount to anything good. I want to kill him for laying his hands upon you. To rip his heart out while it's still beating."

"I know you do my love, but it's alright. I am alright. I was more scared than anything else. The way he was looking at me, like a little girl he could totally control. Knowing whatever he said I must do. And when he got closer, I felt physically ill at the thought that I was powerless against his advances." I single tear slides down the side of my face as my whole-body shivers. Joshua raises his hand to wipe the tear away with his thumb. We lock eyes for a moment and even though there is still anger lingering there, sadness is also visible.

He is upset that I was even in that situation. I have seen some of the women who leave the King's bed chambers. They are always battered and bruised. The complete opposite of how I picture my first time to be.

"I want my first time to be with you Joshua and only you. I didn't even realise until today that he knew who I was. However, from this day forth, I must be careful about what

I say or do around the castle. We don't know who's listening for him."

"I'm just glad you're alright, my love. That you got out of there relatively unscathed and untouched. is a miracle" Joshua pulls me a little closer and moves his head to rest it on my shoulder. He is right. I may have a few marks around my throat and yet that is nothing compared to the other women. I swallow past the fear that rises within me at the thought of what he could have done.

The King is nothing but an abuser. He gets off on hurting women as he sees fit. We are nothing more than a bug stuck under his boot to squish at his will.

"Thank you for coming to find me," I whisper, grabbing his face between my hands and lining it up with mine. His grey eyes shine with unshed tears, and I can't help the small smile that plays on my lips. He gazes at me confused but I ignore it as I move my lips to meet his.

He loves me, it's written all over him and I'll be damned if I'll let the King get in the way of that. I break the kiss just long enough to whisper, "I love you," and move my body around so I'm astride him.

His fingers find their way into my hair, holding me steady as his tongue does wonderous things against mine. I feel him growing beneath me and realise I don't want to wait anymore. I know I promised my mother I would, but I was this close today to having my choices stripped away. I want my first time to be with my love, not with someone who believes they have a right to everything within this realm.

Having made up my mind, I reach down and begin to unbuckle his armour at the side. His kisses become distracted and before I know it, he pulls away.

"Sadie…" He utters while watching my hands move to the buckle on the other side.

"Sshh… It's alright," I release the leather from its strap and raise his blackened armour over his head. Lowering my hands back down to the hem of chain mail, I raise that too, removing it from his body.

"You don't have to do this…" He says stilling my hands. He lowers his head slightly, trying to catch my gaze, "We can still wait," he mentions thoughtfully and yet, I refuse to listen.

"But I don't want to," I lean forward and tug on his padded shirt. I want to see what he looks like underneath. I need to see…

"Sadie, we still have responsibilities to perform." As the last word leaves his mouth images of the Queen flood my brain. Crap!

"Oh no, I'm late," I mutter hastily as I scramble off him and rush towards the door. "I have to go," without even saying goodbye, I open the door and sprint down the hallway. The Queen is going to have my head for this.

8

“Do you care to explain why you’re late?” Queen Sarah stands in the centre of her drawing room with her hands on her hips. She is mad. Who knows when she called for us and by the look on Sophie's face behind her, it was a very long time ago.

“I’m very sorry your Majesty, the King requested my presence after I left here earlier. I was just taking a moment to regain my composure. I am so sorry I’m late.” I say with a slight shake in my voice. The thought of his hand around my throat resurfaces and I begin to blink away my terror. I just need to survive three more months living under this roof, then I shall never have to see him again. But Joshua... would I never be able to see him again either?

“Oh, good heavens child, are you alright?” She looks at me horrified as she walks over to stand directly in front of me. She raises my chin and inspects my eyes. I curse the tear that slides down my face. It’s times like these I wish my mother were here. She always knew what to say to make me feel better.

"Yes, your Majesty," I mutter even though I know the words to be untrue and the Queen does too. She looks upon me, saddened by the thought of her tyrant husband causing me pain.

"Did he hurt you, child?" She whispers and without thinking it through, I slightly nod my head. "How bad?" Her greenish eyes are pleading with me to tell her.

"More mentally than physically ma'am." Her face shows that she still doesn't truly believe me but let's go of my chin. "What did he want from you?" She asks lowering her hands to her sides and walks over to the daybed on the far side of the room. Sophie swiftly brings her some tea before returning to the other side of the daybed. She looks over at me and I know she sees the red welts around my neck because she's staring at them.

"He wanted to know why you sought private council with Father John," I speak a little louder as there is now more distance between us. She goes to take a sip of her tea but then stops.

"And you told him?" She tilts her cup towards her mouth and takes a small sip. Oh, I really hope I did the right thing.

"Unfortunately, yes I did ma'am."

"And what exactly did you say?"

"I told him that you were seeking more protection for her royal Highness, and that Father John told you that the King had it under control.” I stare at her Majesty for a moment and see the corners of her mouth peak up into a slight smile.

“Anything else?” She asks placing her teacup on the table and giving me her full attention. Her long blonde hair looks amazing, glowing in the afternoon sun that's shining through the open window. And she's chosen to wear a beautiful golden sundress which really makes her beauty stand out. The dress matches her new shoes from the Bodega perfectly. It’s as if they were made for each other.

“No, your Majesty, that was all.”

“Very well, thank you, Sadie. Dehlia will be back any second now, I would prefer it if you had the rest of the afternoon off. You have been through enough today. I’ll see you in the morning.” Without waiting for my reply, she leans forward and picks up her book from the centre table. Not wanting to disturb her reading, I quietly curtsy and retreat towards the door. I hear the click of clogs coming towards me and stop just outside the door.

“I can’t believe what you said in there. Are you alright?” Sophie glances at my throat once more and I get the feeling I need to find myself a scarf. I don’t want to attract any unwanted attention.

“No not really, but I will be. I think I’m going to take a walk in the gardens, maybe some fresh air might make me feel better.” I cross my arms over my chest, feeling a tad vulnerable after everything that’s happened. I heard the stories about what the King does but not once in my wildest dreams did it ever cross my mind that it would happen to me.

“That’s a good decision. I’ll be around all afternoon too if you need me. Don’t hesitate, just come.” We hear clogs coming up the hallway and we both glance in their direction. A young girl, maybe fifteen, comes towards us with a pile of logs in her arms. I’m guessing that’s Dehlia, Sophie's replacement.

“Thank you, Sophie, I appreciate it.” She nods and walks back into the Queen's chamber with the young girl in tow. Dehlia’s brown eyes flick towards me as she too nods her head in acknowledgement before crossing over the threshold. I will introduce myself to her properly another time. Right now though, I just need to get out of the confines of this castle.

Dashing down to my chamber, I stumble into my room and quickly change into my casual attire. Out of the corner of my eye, I see the parchment paper sticking out from underneath my cot. Throwing caution to the wind, I decide to take the letters with me into the gardens. Maybe finding out what happened to this mystery person will take my mind off what happened to me.

The sun is warm against my skin as I make it past the gardens and into the meadows on the far side of Castle Rae.

Looking back, I realise just how large the stone structure really is. It looks as if it touches the heavens from this far away. I walk down a rather large embankment until I'm at the base of my favourite tree, on the edge of the Fairwind forest. No one will bother me here.

As a child, I used to sneak away and hide here every time my mother was mad at me. I always waited until sundown to return to her. She was always fuming but happy to see that I was alright.

I sit down and rest my back against the tree trunk. The breeze is chilly against my skin and I'm grateful that I brought my cloak. Leaning back, I raise my head and watch the birds fly around high up in the trees. If only I could be so free.

My mother used to tell me about all the wonderful places she visited when she went travelling with the Queen. My mother was a very loyal woman, she began working for the Queen as soon as she was appointed a maid and never left until the day she died. When I was a child, I wanted to follow in her footsteps, but that all changed when I met Joshua. Now I want a life of my own and in three short months, I might just get it.

There is a loud squawk to my right, and I jump a mile high as a crow perches itself on a log beside me.

"Silly crow, did you have to scare me like that?" I say smiling as I reach into my satchel and pull out a small piece of bread. "Here you go, now on your way." I wait until the bird has gobbled up its food before shooing the inquisitive thing away. I don't need prying eyes for what I'm about to read.

I dig deep into my satchel once more and retrieve the folded-up pieces of parchment. I remove the first one from the small stack and place the rest of them on top of my crossed legs. Peeling the pages away I begin to read...

My Dearest Stephan

You really need to come home. Your brother is causing havoc in our realm. He has promised our people war with the Highlands for not agreeing to his trade agreement. He said that if they won't give us what he wants, then he'll take it by force. My love, you need to stop him. I'm afraid of what he will do next.

He has been trying to court me and I no longer want to reside in Castle Rae. We need to leave, but I need you to return so we can do so.

Please my love, I don't know how much more I can take.

Yours always

Z

From reading this, it appears King Roger was the one who declared war? I thought it was the Highlands who started it all. However, my first recollections from the war are from when I was in my early teens, so I can't really remember. And what does Z mean by the King was courting her? Could these letters be written by her Majesty?

With my heart pounding in my chest, I place the read letter on the ground beside me and pick up another.

My Dearest Stephan

I cannot wait for you anymore, your brother has made his intensions perfectly clear, and I must flee. I will no longer stay under his roof, under his command. He wishes us to wed, and I will not stand for it. I am your wife, and you are my husband. I will never sway from our love, my darling Stephan, but I would rather die than take his hand.

I've decided to leave tomorrow night, after sundown. If you are receiving these letters, meet me when the stars are at their fullest at our usual spot in the Sway. I'll be waiting.

Yours always

Z

Oh my gosh! His Grace has a wife? Why has no one ever mentioned that before? Maybe that's why the King and the Duke had such a falling out. His older brother went after the duchess. But where is she now?

Overcome by sadness for what the Duke and his loving wife have obviously endured, I decide I need a break before continuing. Reaching into my satchel I pull out some cured meats and a small loaf of bread. Cynthia from the kitchens, makes the softest bread in all the realm. The smell alone is like heaven. The crust is hard and yet the middle is beautifully soft, just like a pillow.

I eat in peace, soaking up the suns' rays that filter down through the gaps high up in the trees. The forest is so full of life, not only are there birds moving around from one tree to the next, but I've also seen two deer and one moose grazing amongst the foliage on the forest floor.

It's so serene out here, I often forget that there is a whole other life outside of the stone structure way back yonder. I wish I didn't have to go back. King Roger comes to mind and the thought of him alone makes me lose my appetite. Placing my remaining food back inside my satchel, I rearrange my position and pick up the next letter.

My Darling Stephan

I write to you today not with happy news but with sadness. Your brother learnt about my plans to flee and cornered me as I was passing through the castle gates. He threatened to behead us both if I ever try such nonsense again.

My love, I no longer care for my safety however, I care for yours. Only the angels know where you are right now as it's been two months since you left.

It feels like forever.

The messengers told me they delivered my letters to your comrades and yet you still don't reply. I fear this will be my last letter, my love. I doubt your brother will allow me to continue to write to you once we are wed.

Just know that I'm sorry my love and that I will love you forever.

Yours always

Z

Z has to be her Majesty, Queen Sarah! King Roger has only ever had one wife. Oh my gosh the revelation, I see now what they are fighting for. Why the Duke has never stopped his advances on Castle Rae. He doesn't want the throne; he wants his wife. And yet, this isn't the last letter either. There are two or three more back in my chambers. I must read them...

Staggering to my feet, I pull my cloak tightly around my body as the late afternoon sun fades behind the mountains. I was so engrossed in the letters that I had no idea it had gotten so late. It would be close to supper time by now.

Making my way up the embankment I hear chatter coming from my left and quickly duck down, covering my head with my cloak. It's not a crime to be out this far but it is a crime to be out this late. No one is allowed outside after sundown.

"... oh and the sound of Rod's neck snapping in two, that completely made my day." A grungy voice declares gleefully, making my stomach do somersaults. How could someone be so happy about someone else's death?

I hear the clink of metal armour not too far away and I know that these are no ordinary patrolmen, they are either knights or the King's own personal guards. Moving my body lower, I lie flat against the damp ground and prey that they don't see me while they walk by.

"Yeah, that bastard had it coming to him too. The guy nearly killed me the other week when we caught him camping out in the woods." In the woods? I thought they found him in the Sway. "Oh, I forgot to tell you too, He looked right at me yesterday before the executioner popped the bag over his head. I couldn't help but smile knowing that he was there instead of us." What did he just say!?

The crunching of footsteps sounds no more than five metres away and I will my body into stillness. My cloak is similar to that of the colour of the grass, and they would have to look directly at me to see me. The only problem is my body is a mound on a rather flat embankment.

"I second that, I thought it was perfect timing too, finding Rod the day before we executed the Kings plan. Now, Stephan will see that he is no match when it comes to what his brother is prepared to do." They were the ones who killed those people in the Sway? Not Rod? Why didn't he say anything yesterday before the hanging? I suddenly remember his last words and a shiver runs down my spine. "The Duke wants what's rightfully his and is willing to do whatever it takes to get it."

"No match indeed," The second guard says proudly as they pass by. I hold my breath as the grass crunches under their heavy boots. They are so close now that if one of them were to look down, I'd be a goner.

“Only two more days until we execute project princess. Are you ready?” Oh my gosh, are they going to attack the princess? Is this what the Queen is so worried about?

“Man, I was born ready. Also, I can’t wait to see how the Queen will react to this one. She’s already on high alert since the attack on the Sway. I have a weird feeling she knows it was us too and not the Duke. She’s been acting rather odd since the day it happened.”

“Well wouldn’t you, your people were killed only days after you toured their grounds. I doubt that she knows though, the order was given to those of us who truly follow the King. That’s why pretty boy Joshua was left out of the mission. His head is so far up her arse that he could probably see out of her mouth.” I hear the laughter in the grungy soldier's voice and want to smack him for his snide remark. How dare he say such things about Joshua!

“Ha ha, man that’s so wrong.”

“Isn’t it the truth though? He is always being summoned to her chambers. It wouldn’t surprise me if it came out that he was bedding her. Especially with how late she calls for him.”

“The guy is a prune, I doubt he would even know how to use his equipment, unlike us. I would give the Queen the ride of a lifetime.”

“For what, a whole two minutes?” The younger guard laughs while his footsteps become faster and it sounds as if he is running away. Their voices fade off into the distance and I brave a small peak from underneath my hood.

Looking up, I see that the coast is clear and remove my hood entirely.

Dusk has surely settled, and stars now begin to speckle in the night sky. I have to get to the dining hall before anyone wonders where I am. Getting up on all fours I look over the ridge and down to the right. Far in the distance, I see two stocky shadows moving further down the patrolman's path. Quickly scrambling up to the level ground, I tuck my satchel into my side and sprint off towards the castle.

9

"I need to talk to you," I whisper into Joshua's ear as I take my seat at the table beside him. I glance over at the Queen and see a worried expression cross her face as she converses with her husband. If only she knew what is going to happen in the next two days. I must warn her, but how? I don't even know all the facts. All I know is that the King is planning something and if those soldiers really were the ones who attacked the Sway, this is going to be bad.

"Where have you been? Supper is almost over!" Joshua scowls, making me feel like a small child. He half turns his body towards me and ducks his head so he can get a better look. His grey eyes roam my body, looking for any sign that something is amiss. I should have paid more attention to the setting sun. Of course, Joshua is on edge after what the King did to me earlier today.

"I was out in the Fairwind Forest. I got so lost in the words written in the letters you gave me that I lost track of time."

"The forest? ..." Joshua speaks a little too loudly, making the people around us turn their heads to see what all the fuss is about. Realising his mistake, he returns his stare to face forward and eats the last few vegetables remaining on his plate. "You know you're not allowed out there after dark," He says, not taking his eyes off his dish.

"I'm aware and I know it was a mistake." I glance at the people sitting next to me and see that they are no longer interested in what is going on between us. They've all gone back to their wines and the constant banter going on between those around them.

"Please try not to do it again, I won't be able to protect you if you break the law." Joshua reaches for his gauntlet and takes a huge swig. I watch a drop of crimson wine slide down the side of his stubbled cheek and hit the ground beside him and realise the entire dining hall has broken out into song to farewell a fellow Knight who's chosen to take his maiden and leave Castle Rae.

I don't know why but I glance over at the King and see an angry glower on his face. He's obviously not happy about the news of yet another soldier leaving his ranks. What sort of image does that show the rest of our region, that our people would rather spend their days ploughing fields than guarding our gates?

"Understood," I whisper under my breath as I lean forward and dig into my mash potatoes. Although with the news I overheard today, I am not hungry but eat anyway, not knowing when I will get my next meal. I have no idea what project princess entails, but I will be damned if I let myself go hungry because of it.

Joshua leans back in his chair and throws his arm over the back of mine. He looks so relaxed as he glances around the room, smiling at those who catch his eye. He really is a lovable Knight. It's not very often that you hear of a man in this realm who treats people equally and fairly.

Joshua places his right leg over his thigh and leans back a little bit more before taking another swig out of his gauntlet. He wipes his mouth clean with the back of his hand and rests his arm upon his bended knee.

"Now, what did you want to talk about?" I'm stunned for a moment as I don't know where to begin and decide this probably isn't the best place for this conversation.

"It's best if we discuss this in private," I take a bite of the roasted chicken and internally moan at how good it is. Cynthia really is an absolutely, amazing cook.

"Very well. I have to do something to attend to first, but I can meet you in your chambers after." He says quietly and I slightly nod my head.

Without another word, Joshua places his gauntlet on the table and leaves the room. People have gathered to dance and sing between the grand tables and normally I would smile at such an event but today I just can't. My worries are sickening me, and I have to force myself to swallow every bite. I raise my gauntlet to my lips while I peer across the room and accidentally lock eyes with the devil. His nauseating grin almost makes all the food in my stomach rise.

No wonder 'Z' was so afraid of him becoming King. How could we all be so blinded to think that Duke Stephan is the evil one in this situation? It's the King who is scaring us into submission. We are all little lambs following the orders of a wolf.

He puckers his lips towards me, and I immediately turn my eyes away. I really have to be more careful. Who knows what the King would have done to me if I was caught outside after dark? The last person who was, received ten lashings in the courtyard. I fear my punishment would have been severely worse.

"You all right there Sadie? You look like you've seen a ghost." Lance asks from further down the table. I glance over at him and give him a small smile.

"Yes, sorry, I'm just not feeling too well. I think I'm going to call it a night." I wipe the corners of my mouth with my napkin before placing it on the table. The heavy wooden chair scrapes along the ground as I push it back and stand up. Lance eyes me warily before letting go of whatever else he was about to say.

"I hope you feel better in the morning." He says sincerely as I pass him and head towards the door. It's been a very long day and I'm in dire need of sleep but there is one thing I need to discuss first.

10

“When did you know about the attack on the Sway?” I blurt out the moment Joshua enters my room and closes the door. He stands there staring at me confused with his hand still on the handle.

“Why do you ask?” He says cautiously while moving away from the door. He walks over to where I’m standing in the corner of the room but keeps his distance, stopping about three feet away.

“Just answer the question!” I snap and his eyes go wide. I have never been so forceful in all the years he has known me. Hopefully, seeing me this way, he knows I mean business.

I watch him for a moment as his eyes roam up and down my body. His back has gone ridged and the mood in the room has changed into something darker. His eyes are full of desire as he gazes down at me like a hunter stalking his prey.

“Well?” I ask crossing my arms over my chest. I’m in no mood for the distraction or the delay. He needs to tell me right now before I kick him out of my chambers.

His eyebrows flick up and a small smile plays on his lips. I’m getting the impression that he is proud of me for my performance.

“Alright, let me think... I believe I was informed late afternoon, on the day it happened. One of the guards from the wall was telling everyone.”

“So, you knew nothing about it before?”

“What? Why would I?” Joshua mirrors my stance and I see the anger rising in his eyes.

The information the soldiers revealed earlier, along with their comments about Joshua when they thought no one was listening, gives me no rise to second guess my choice to trust him but he is still a Knight in the King's army no less, so I really hope what I'm about to disclose doesn't backfire in my face.

“What I have to tell you must not leave this room. The reason I was late for supper is that I was almost caught by two of the King's personal guards.”

“Are you kidding me, Sadie?” Joshua tightens the grip on his biceps, turning his knuckles white.

“Be quiet and listen! After packing up my things, I was walking up the embankment and heard people heading my way. I covered myself with my cloak and ducked down. They were discussing the death of Rod Fern and mentioned how he was taking the fall for what they did."

"What?!" Joshua seethes quietly as his stance turns deadly. I see now the true Knight that lays within him. Not only the one of strength, bravery and skill but also the one of death and destruction.

"They also mentioned that there is going to be another attack. Something they called project princess."

"Sard!..." He swears loudly and begins pacing the room. He says things under his breath that I cannot hear before he returns and stops directly in front of me again, but this time closer. I feel his breath hitting my cheek every time he exhales. Long gone is the feeling of confidence within me. I suddenly feel like a scared little fawn under the watchful gaze of a hunter. "Did they say when it's coming?" He asks through gritted teeth.

"In two days," I say with a shaky breath, trying to swallow past the lump that's formed in my throat. I'm cornered with nowhere to run, and although I know he would never attack or hurt me, I'm still extremely uncomfortable with the anger radiating off of him.

"You've told no one else?" He says peering down from above.

"No one," I whisper.

"Good, keep it that way." Without another word, he turns on his heels and stalks back towards the closed door. He places his hand on the handle and halts. Turning his gaze towards me, his features fade into sadness as he opens his mouth to speak. “You must not let anyone know that you know. For your own safety and mine, please act as if everything is normal.” He doesn’t wait for my reply as he opens the door and walks out.

I’m saddened by the fact this news feels like it's put a rift between us. We were finally getting to a place where we were relaxed and could be ourselves.

Stepping up to the small table next to my cot, I pick up my gauntlet and take a huge gulp. Water cascades down my throat, hydrating it as it goes. Joshua’s reaction to my news has put me on edge. I’m certain that he didn’t know about the attack on the Sway before it happened, but the depth of his temper definitely rattled me. Hopefully, he can find out what project princess is all about and stop it before it happens. Only time will tell.

11

The next day is a blur, filled with a list of duties and chores that the Queen has us doing. With Sophie training Dehlia, I am left to doing all the cleaning and washing up after each event.

"That will be all for today ladies. I will see myself to bed." Queen Sarah announces from her bedroom. She is still in the lovely silver gown that she wore for supper and although I know she told us to leave, she usually requires some help to get out of it.

"Yes, Your Majesty however your dress," I mutter quietly knowing I'm stepping a little out of line.

"You needn't worry about that Sadie. I will see to it myself. You may leave."

"Yes, your Majesty. Good night." I curtsy and leave the room, shutting the door behind me. Her guards stand to attention the moment I walk past, and I just smile at them. It was a very busy day, and I am exhausted. I can't wait to climb into bed and sleep off the anxiety that's built up within me. That's if I can sleep. Last night all I did was toss and turn, the guard's declaration playing over and over in my head.

The hallways are empty as I make my way back to my quarters. Only those who are still working at this time of night are seen walking about. I hear quick footsteps down the next passageway and wish they would slow down. It's probably a maid running late to return to her duties. We've all been there.

The full moon shines through the openings in the wall and I bask in its glory as I walk by. It's a rare sight to see the moon during our wet season. The courtyard below is eerily quiet as only a handful of guards patrol the perimeter, always ready for when the next attack might be. If only they knew that the next one will most likely come from the inside.

I see a few guards grouped up ahead and begin to slow my pace. What are they doing? I think to myself. Four of them, clad in blackened out armour surround what I can only assume is a small female. One of the guards lets out a disturbing chuckle and my legs begin to freeze. Oh my gosh… What are they doing?

"Look lads, another missy wants a piece of the action." The guard on the far side has lifted his head and is now staring directly at me. My whole body has gone ridged, and I can no longer move.

"Ohh, and she's a pretty one too." Another guard has turned his gaze towards me and bites his lower lip as his eyes roam all over my body. Swallowing my fear, I take a hesitant step back and raise my shaky arms.

"I don't want any trouble."

"It's too late for that sweety, trouble has found you... GET HER!" The guard on the far side announces and at his command, the other three break away and begin to head towards me. They reveal a scared Dehlia with her eyes swollen from tears. She looks directly at me while the older guard has his hand wrapped around her throat. I feel horrible for leaving her behind, but I am of no use to her if they catch me too.

My feet move at lightning speed as I run back the way I came, down towards the Queen's chambers. I hear the clank of metal not far behind as the three guards begin to close in. Forgoing the punishment that will await me for yelling. I begin to scream.

"HELP!!!... SOMEBODY, PLEASE HELP!!!" I round the next corner, into the Queen's hallway and crash into something hard. "Ow!"

Lifting my gaze I stare up into the most hate filled eyes I have ever seen.

"There she is. Just the wee lass we've been looking for." Lance says in his brogue accent. His sneer is unmissable, even in the dim lighting.

"No, I'm not." I blurt out before realising it would probably be best if I didn't say anything at all.

"Oh yes, you are. The King's been expecting you." He leans forward and grabs me by my hair. A high pitch screech leaves my mouth as he pulls me to my feet. Once I'm standing, two brutes from behind grab ahold of my forearms and push me forward.

We travel through the long passageways until we reach a huge metal door. Lance steps forward and knocks three times, waits for a moment, and then repeats the gesture. The door swings wide open, allowing us entry to travel through.

The gardens look almost magical against the moon that shines high above. We pass the Queen's favourite rosemary bush as we make our way down towards the armoury in the far corner of the castle.

A few worried onlookers catch my gaze and I plead with my eyes that they seek shelter. I do not have the slightest clue what is happening, but I do not want anyone else caught in the crossfire.

Glancing over my right shoulder I see three guards, and over my left, there are four. Seven guards, including those who have bound my arms travel behind me with another three in front, including the biggest traitor of all. I thought Lance was our friend, but it seems he was double crossing us this whole time. I hope he wasn't the one who Joshua turned to for help. Maybe that's what this is all about.

Maybe Joshua told him about project princess and that is why they came for me.

My terror spikes anew when we near the armoury's steal gates and I see King Roger seething on the other side.

"I don't care how long it will take! FIND HIM!!" King Roger roars and three guards march out of the barracks heading back towards the castle. I wish I were going with them and not into hell itself. I'm terrified, not knowing what the King has in store for me?

As we pass over the threshold I try and plant my feet firmly into the ground. However, the men behind me are ten times stronger than I will ever be and continue to force me forward.

"Your Majesty, Sadie Jaymes." Lance steps to the side allowing the King to have a clear view of me. The King's eyes light up in amazement as the guards behind me push me forward and I slip, falling to my knees.

"Well done lads. Part one of my plan is already in motion. Now for phase two. String her up."

"What? No! Your Majesty, I haven't done anything wrong. I did what you asked." I say pleadingly as I press my hands together and bow my head before my King. I cannot die by hanging. I just can't. A tear slides down the side of my cheek as my body begins to uncontrollably shake, giving away just how scared I really am.

King Roger pulls me to my feet by my hair, "SHUT UP!!" he yells in my face. "This night is not about you." He lets go of my hair and pushes me towards the guards standing near the open door.

"South side, they've moved." Is the only thing King Roger says before I'm whisked away. I thrash against their hold, trying anything I can to break free, but it doesn't work. They haul me up the great stairs leading to the top of the castle wall. Fires are lit the whole way along and guards with bows and arrows fill every nook. I'm carted over to an extremely large opening on the far righthand side and placed dead centre.

Tears are streaming down my face as I turn to the guard closest to me. "Please don't do this. I'll do anything. Just please let me go." I whimper in defeat. The guard before me chuckles as he leans down and picks up the rope by his feet. He toys with the end as he nods and the guard behind me forces my left arm into the air. It's only now that I see that I am not going to be hung to death, but worse. I am to be strung up by my hands and feet, high in the air for the world to see.

"No... No, no, no. Please stop." I beg and yet they ignore me. They make quick work tying the knots around my wrists before moving to secure the ropes around my ankles. The guard in front of me even chuckles with glee as pain ignites in my arms and legs as I'm hoisted off the ground and into the air. Screams of anguish leave my body even though I know no one near me cares. Why are they doing this to me? What did I do?

Out past the castle walls and into the meadows is a camp filled with tents, as far as the eye can see. Fires are lit all around, displaying the grand size. There would have to be over two hundred soldiers down there. Has Duke Stephan finally arrived? Or is this the Highlands once more?

"On my count," A soldier says from somewhere below on the castle wall. "Ready," Oh my gosh, they are going to open fire with me strung up here. "Aim," He calls out and I squeeze my eyes shut, not wanting to witness the death that will surely occur in the next few seconds. "FIRE!" He bellows and the sound of bow strings releasing their arrows is unmistakable before being replaced by the noise of wood flying through the air.

My heart stops and I hear the sound of the first arrow hitting its target with a definite thunk. Then multiple follow suit. I shudder as I realise multiple people will die tonight.

Deeming the first wave over, I open my eyes. So many soldiers line the grounds below and I become sick with dread as I see them readying their arrows, aiming towards us.

"HOLD YOUR FIRE!" Someone below shouts and I feel my body sag with relief. Thank the heavens. Those beyond the castle wall have stilled their weapons as someone from the front has broken rank to run back towards the camp.

"Looks like they took the bait lads. Ready your bows." The commander says behind me. Am I the bait? The sound of bow strings arching beneath me makes me want to throw up. They cannot be serious. The enemy isn't fighting back!

“Aim!” Oh, no.

“FIRE!” The commander screams and I close my eyes once more. The sound of arrows ricocheting off of a shield is a much better sound than plunging deep into a warm body. My muscles ache from the pain and I want nothing more than to run away from this place. To flee Castle Rae and never return.

After a while, it feels like hours have passed and I begin to weep. I can no longer bear what the King is forcing me to endure. The pain in my arms and legs is excruciating and I no longer want to open my eyes. Instead, I start thinking it maybe be better if an arrow was to find its way into my heart. At least then there'd be no more pain!

“THE DUKE SEEKS AN AUDIENCE WITH THE KING!” Someone shouts from beyond the wall and my eyes spring open. It’s the Duke, he’s here.

“About time,” The commander says below me on the wall. I hear him walking away and then out of the blue he stops. “You two, get her down. She’s coming with us.” He says to the two soldiers standing closest to me. My fear spikes anew at his words. Not because I will be released from my bindings, which I’m thankful for but because I'm scared that I will once again have to endure the presence of the King. Gosh, I wish this night was over.

12

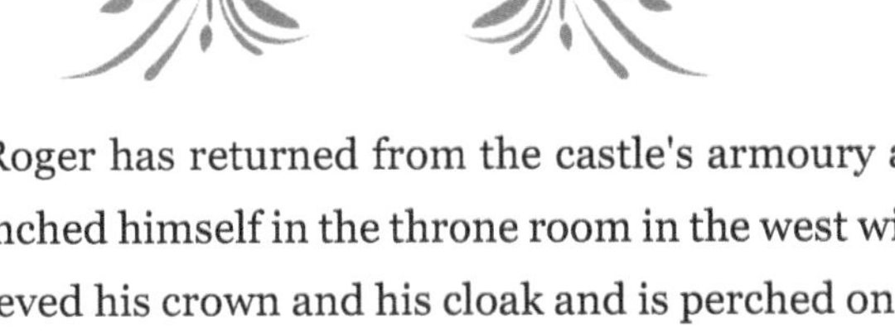

King Roger has returned from the castle's armoury and has entrenched himself in the throne room in the west wing. He's retrieved his crown and his cloak and is perched on his throne like the tyrant he is. His beady eyes roam all around, watching and waiting for his dear younger brother to show his face.

I notice that he has also woken the castle's nobility, making sure they are all present to bear witness to whatever is about to take place. Turning my gaze upon them, I see that they all seem to have been dressed in a hurry. All except for the Queen that is. She is still in her beautiful silver gown, the one she wore to supper. What has she been doing all this time? Did she know this was going to happen? Is that why she didn't want us to undress her?

Queen Sarah's eyes flick towards me as a sad smile plays on her lips. She half turns away and whispers something quietly to a messenger standing beside her, once he's heard all he needs to hear, he dashes off quickly out of the room.

Princess Hayley, on the Queen's other side, appears to still be asleep as she leans her head against her mother's shoulder. Queen Sarah scolds her daughter for behaving poorly but she doesn't listen. What else is new?

The great metal doors at the end of the throne room boom as they swing wide open, allowing the Duke and his men to enter.

"Brother!" King Roger announces happily, however we all know it's an illusion. He is trying to show that he is the victor in all this.

"Cut the crap, Roger!" The Duke spits angrily as he comes to a stop at the base of the dais. "Just give her back and I'll be on my way. No one else has to get hurt." The Duke's guards gaze around the room, all ready to jump when the order is given, but so are the King's men. I stand between two companies of soldiers ready to fight when the time is right. This is not somewhere I want to be.

I see Joshua enter from the side door and my heart picks up as he walks closer to me. I may no longer have the restraints around my limbs, but they have been replaced by big red welts. Joshua's eyes roam my body and I see his eyes turn dark as he stares at the marks around my ankles. He stops just out of reach as his eyes travel up and down one last time before he whispers, "Are you alright?" Not wanting to show that we are talking, I slightly nod my head and turn my attention back to the centre of the room.

“But she is no longer your's brother. She has become mine.” King Roger leans forward on his throne and glares down at his brother.

“Bullshit! She was never yours. Now give her back.”

“Did you like my little show before?” Roger asks, deflecting the request from the Duke. Stephan looks baffled for a moment before his gaze swings over to me. “You always did have a thing for the help.” The Duke’s eyes turn sad as he too sees the red welts around my ankles. He saw what the King was doing to me earlier and stopped the fight. He is a bigger man than his brother will ever be. Anger returns to his eyes as he turns his attention back to the throne.

“You’re pathetic brother. You always have been and always will be. Mother knew it, I knew it, hell, all of Castle Rae knows it. You would rather instil fear in everyone instead of ruling Castle Rae as it should be. I’ve seen your work down in the Sway, how you ration their food supply just so you can hold banquets here every evening. Cutting off their access to water once a month just to please some sick part of yourself.

Only a fool would believe that I killed all those people months ago. You murdered them and captured my friend just so you had somewhere else to place the blame. Hell, you even risked the life of this poor lass just to stop us from attacking your precious castle.” Stephan's gaze swiftly shifts over to me once more before returning to his brother.

“You don’t care for the people, you only care about your position on the throne. But I’m here to tell you, I’m here to tell all of you. I don't want the throne. I never have. I just want what's mine and then I'll be on my way. You will never have to hear from me ever again." Murmurs erupt throughout the crowds within the room and the King's eyes turn deadly. He looks over his left shoulder to a guard standing not too far away and gives him a slight nod.

For a moment the man doesn't move, he just stands there as still as a statue with his eyes locked on the other side of the room. As the King begins to speak, he slowly walks over to whatever has caught his attention.

"Do you really think after all this time that I'm just going to hand her over? You really mustn't know me at all brother!" The King says through gritted teeth as his guard picks up his pace. Within a flash, Princess Hayley's head is ripped away from her mother's shoulder and a knife is pressed against her throat. Her eyes go wide as she stares at the man she calls father. The Duke looks confused as he witnesses the commotion unfolding in front of him.

"ROGER! NO! PLEASE," Queen Sarah screams as another guard steps forward to pull the Queen back away from her daughter.

"What is going on?... Father?... Why are you doing this?" Princess Hayley says with a shaky breath. She turns her head slightly to look at her mother before returning her gaze to the throne.

The King has a triumphant expression on his face, believing he has won. He slouches back in his throne and raises his chin, staring down his nose at all of us. His greyish black hair peaks out from underneath his crown, showing us his real age. His lips are slightly upturned into a smirk, and I see his blue eyes gazing victoriously down at his brother.

"Many years ago, I encouraged our father to send Stephan away to help the Sway. There was an unruly matter happening down there and I could not be bothered dealing with it myself. Knowing that father wanted to abdicate the throne, I convinced him to move the date forward just after Stephan had left. With my brother out of the way, there was no one around to question my right to rule.

My mother however didn't approve of my stancher and tried everything she could to stop the coronation. Even went as far as hiding my father's crown. But as soon as I was King, I got rid of the old bat. I didn't need her beady eyes staring at me every time I entered a room." The entire room gasps as the King finally admits to killing his own mother. Legend has it that she killed herself by jumping out of the fourth story window, however now we know the truth.

"I knew you had something to do with mother!" Duke Stephan seethes as he takes a menacing step forward. He wraps his fingers even tighter around the hilt of his sword, making them turn white.

"Guilty." The King says with a glimmer of humour in his voice. "Then with mother and father out of the way, your delicious young wife was mine for the taking. I courted her for weeks before forcing her hand. She always was a feisty little thing. Never did anything she was told. But it wasn't until the night before the wedding that I found out my dashing bride-to-be was with child." Another round of gasps erupts from those around me, and I glance over at the Queen. Her eyes are pleading with the guard standing behind her daughter, but he doesn't care. He has his orders, and will not break rank for anyone but the King.

"Child?" The Duke whispers as his head turns towards the Princess. "It can't be." He shifts his gaze to the floor in front of him, appearing to be deep in thought. He stares at the open space for a moment before glancing towards the Queen. She looks as if she's holding back tears as she slightly nods her head.

"And Zalia?" The Duke asks although I think he already knows the answer. The King was speaking about his lover in the past tense and that can only mean one thing.

"Dead." This is the only word spoken by the Queen before the Duke hangs his head in sorrow. His men behind him slightly relax their guard as they are saddened by the sudden announcement. So many years have been spent fighting for the Duke's stolen love, only to find out that she has been dead this whole time.

"NOW!" The King bellows and all the guards lining the walls jump forward and attack those in the middle of the room. Blades clack together as they whirl around in a flurry of movement. The guard with the knife to the Princess's throat swipes right, slicing through her windpipe. He drops her to the ground before rushing to join the others.

“HAYLEY!” The Queen’s painful screams fill the room as the Duke's eyes go wide with shock. He watches helplessly as his only daughter grabs at her throat while her blood spills out all over the floor in front of her. His eyes turn angrily towards his brother and a hate filled expression crosses his face.

“I’M GOING TO DESTROY YOU!!” The Duke roars before launching forward. King Roger shoots to his feet as his personal guard's swarm in to protect him. I, however, am too stunned to move as I witness all the chaos unfolding in front of me.

A moment later, I feel his warmth all around me. “I have to get you out of here,” Joshua says as he grabs a hold of my right bicep and begins to pull me over towards the huge metal doors leading out of the room.

“But the Queen,” Is all I can muster as I risk a glance behind me and see her loyal guards coming to her rescue. Tears stream down my face as I watch them pull her away kicking and screaming as she tries to cling to her daughter’s lifeless body. I can only imagine the pain she is experiencing right now. She may not have been the Queen’s biological daughter, but she's raised and obviously still cared for her as if she were her own.

We barely make it over the threshold before Joshua slides in front of me and is about to throw me over his shoulder. I’m about to question him why, but as I lift my head, I see three of the King’s men chasing after us and shake my head. Instead, I firmly take hold of his hand and shout, "run". We both know Joshua's long legs can move way faster than mine but carrying me will only slow us down.

"We just need to make it to the tunnels," Joshua says more to himself than I and begins to pick up pace, sprinting faster towards the maid's quarters and the secret tunnels that lie beyond. Only a handful of people know about the tunnels built under the main stairwell and it's for a good reason.

The Queen showed me the tunnels and entrances on the very first day I became her lady's maid. Not all maids and guards have the privilege to know of their existence. The tunnels were designed by the Queen herself and built under total secrecy by her trusted confidants on the off chance that she ever needed an escape route. Never in a million years did I think I'd be escaping through them!

With Joshua leading the way, he has managed to give us a small window of opportunity from those following us. We round the next corner, and he heads towards the last room on the left and slams the door shut behind us. Dashing over to the far wall, he quickly draws back the cupboard's doors and shoves me inside.

"I'll find you." He says and then places a sweet kiss on my lips and shuts the doors. It's dark in here and my heart is beating erratically against my rib cage.

"There is nowhere you can hide that we won't find you, Knight." The sound of voices filter in through the room beyond and I know that I'm running out of time. As quietly as I can, I move the cloaks out of the way and feel around for the latch that will release the opening to the secret passage. I hear their footsteps getting closer just as my fingers grasp the metal handle. YES! Turning the handle down, the door swings inwards and I quickly stumble through. With haste, I quietly shut the door and block it off with the slab of wood lying beside me. Only those looking for the latch will know it's there, so for the time being I'm safe.

The wood is cold against my legs, but I don't risk getting to my feet. It's almost pitch black, with the only light shining through the cracks in the walls. Crawling forward, I remember the path I've moved through many times before. The Queen made me train and practice the route over and over so that I would know the way by memory alone. Fourteen steps forward then turn right, twenty-seven steps forward then turn left...

I have this whole labyrinth mapped out in my brain and am thankful to the Queen for showing me the way. If it wasn't for her, we I would probably have been captured by those mad men chasing after us. But why were they chasing after me? That doesn't make any sense. Maybe it was Joshua they were after. He is a notorious Knight after all. I do hope he's alright, but I won't know until I get out of here though. So, I keep moving. Eighteen steps forward...

13

The breeze is cold against my face as I open the wooden hatch door deep within the Fairwind forest. Sunlight filters down through the trees as I take in a huge gulp of fresh air. It took me hours of crawling to get through the tunnels leading out of Castle Rae. My hands and knees are bruised to the bone. Only the heavens know what has transpired since I've been gone.

I hear chatter coming from somewhere on my right, so as quietly as I can I shut the hatch door and cover it up with fallen leaves. You never know who is out here in the woods and I don't want them stumbling across the entrance. I duck behind a huge tree and peer around it to see two men dressed in the Duke's armour. They are relieving themselves against another tree less than fifty feet away. Do I trust them? Can I trust them? Deciding I have no other options, I wait until they are finished before revealing myself. I don't want to startle them and risk seeing more than I'd like, thank you very much!

“I mean you no harm,” I state confidently, while stepping forward and raising my hands beside my head. I almost stumble forward as my shoe gets caught on a hidden branch. I really should watch where I'm walking.

“Who goes there? Don’t move!” Both the guards yell in unison as they aim their weapons at my head. Fear like never before shoots through me and my life flashes before my eyes as I think they're about fire on me.

The guards gaze upon me like predators would their prey and yet, out of the blue they glance towards each other. I watch as one of them mouths. ‘It’s the girl from the wall.’ They both have this look of wonderment upon their faces as they glance back over at me. What’s that about? Not wanting to wait to find out, I begin to speak, “My name is Sadie Jaymes. I am one of the Queen’s lady's maids and I seek an audience with his Grace.” Hopefully, this will make them lower their weapons. Only the angels know what I’m going to do or say once I meet the Duke, but I’ll cross that ravine when it comes.

“You seek an audience with his Grace? Whatever for?” The guard on the right questions while raising his brows.

“Queen's business. You do not need to know.” I say lowering my arms and crossing them over my chest. I’m trying to portray that I mean business, instead of a scared little girl walking around with her tail between her legs. I really hope they don’t call my bluff.

“Really? Well, we can’t argue with that. Come on then.” Both men lower their weapons and turn around, heading back to the camp that's not too far in the distance. I can't believe that worked.

Not wanting to be left behind, I dash to catch up with them and begin to match their stride. There are hundreds of soldiers out here, so I'm guessing the fight within Castle Rae is over or they reluctantly retreated. Hopefully, I'll find out which one it is soon enough. I just hope Joshua is alright.

We pass by what I can only presume is the medical tent. The smell of burnt flesh hits my nose and I have to force myself to swallow the bile that rises in my throat. I hear the grunts and moans from the wounded soldiers, but I don't dare look. I can't, for if I do, they will be my undoing. I would drop my mission to see the Duke, to find safety for myself and to hopefully provide aid wherever I am able to do so. But for now, I must find out what is going on.

"He's in there." The guard on the left points to the largest tent in the middle of the camp. Of course, he is... Where else would he be?

"Thank you," I utter calmly as I walk past them at a brisk pace towards the tent. I really hope I know what I'm doing. There are two guards holding spear axes manning the entrance. As I make my approach their spears clash together barring my passage.

"Your business here?" One of them says under heavy hooded armour.

"I'm here by order of the Queen." I raise my head a little higher and hope they do not turn me away. I still have no idea what I'm going to say to the grieving man, but I hope I can bring him some sort of peace. I grew up with Hayley and even though we were never really friends, I knew absolutely everything there was to know about her.

"Let her in," A booming voice filters out from within the tent and my back goes stiff at the sound. He sounds angrier than I expected and makes me second guess my decision to come here. Before I have a chance to think, the guards raise their spears and on unsteady legs, I walk through the open flaps.

His Grace is leaning over a huge wooden desk in the middle of the room, glancing down at a map laid out on the table. There are lanterns lit all around and a huge four-poster bed sits on the far side of the room. Other than that, the room is basically bare. Not what I expected at all for the Duke's tent.

"Who are you child and why did Sarah send you?" He asks without ever taking his eyes off the map.

"My name is Sadie Jaymes your Grace, and I am sorry, but I lied. The Queen never sent me. I escaped the incident in the throne room and didn't know where else to go."

"And your first thought was to come here?" He slightly snarks at me. Maybe he is more like his brother than I originally thought. The letters that his late wife wrote however, make me believe otherwise.

"Not exactly, your soldiers caught me off guard in the forest. It was either show myself, or risk getting shot." He raises his eyes in disbelief at my bluntness. A small smirk teases at the corner of his mouth while he moves to straighten up.

“I admire your bravery, Sadie. I once knew a woman who was just like you, in more ways than one.” The Duke’s voice lingers with sorrow as he hangs his head. His eyes have turned sad and I know he is thinking about his fallen lover.

“I’m sorry about your wife... and your daughter too.” I end my sentence with a whisper. His grief-stricken eyes look up at me and I am crushed by the sadness I see. This man has fought black and blue to get to those he loves most. Only to find out that his wife is dead and to have his daughter ripped away from him before he even had the chance to know her.

He nods his head, “I accept your condolences however, I must apologise too,”

“Whatever for your Grace?” I say placing a hand over my heart. What in this realm has this man got to be sorry for?

“For the way my brother treated you. No matter your stature within the walls of Castle Rae, no one deserves to be strung up like that.” After what happened recently, I had almost forgotten about the incident on the wall. How is that even possible considering the pain I endured? Looking down, I sneak a peek at the fat red welts around my wrists. I have no doubt these will turn into very nasty bruises.

Without another word, I nod my thanks. A lump has formed in my throat, making it impossible for me to speak. The Duke notices how the conversation is making me uncomfortable and goes back to pondering over his map without saying anything else.

I glance around the tent and notice a few things on the floor, right next to the desk. The King's shield lies upside down with blood splattered all over the inside.

"Did you kill him?" I blurt out, forgetting formalities. The Duke doesn't bother to raise his eyes as he says, "Unfortunately, no. The slimy mongrel managed to evade us. While we were busy fighting his personal guards, he slipped out the back and ordered more soldiers into the throne room. We were able to retreat just in time to save most of our men." The Duke places a pawn in the centre of the map and moves another to the far side.

"I'm glad you were able to get out but what will you do now, Your Grace?"

"We are just waiting for the sign. It should be here any moment." As if on cue, the tent flaps open wide and in strolls Joshua.

"You made it," He declares, as he rushes forward and scoops me up into his arms, whirling me around the room as if we are the only two people in the room. "I was so worried when I didn't hear anything. In saying that though, I would never have thought to check the Duke's tent. This is honestly the last place I thought I'd find you." He sets me back on my feet and places a smooth loving kiss upon my lips. I'm so glad he's alright. I've been worried sick.

“Good, you’re both acquainted.” The Duke says from behind me and my stomach drops. For a moment I completely forgot where we were.

“Your Grace I ...” I begin but he raises his hand stopping my sentence.

“There is no need child. I am fully aware of the connection you have with my son. I am just happy to see you both made it out unscathed.” A small, but sad smile plays on his lips as he stands to his full height. His Son? As I stare at Joshua and then back at the Duke, I believe I’m starting to see the resemblance. How did I not see it before? His shaggy hair, the straightness of his back, his deep grey eyes, it’s all there staring back at me. But then again, no one in the castle has physically seen the Duke in years, so how could I have possibly noticed any comparison?

“Sadie...” Joshua begins, and I return my attention to the man standing before me. “For years I’ve wanted to tell you who I was, but Queen Sarah thought it would be unwise for anyone else to know the truth.

You see, my parents had me out of wedlock and as you well know, that is highly frowned upon within the courts. So, before anyone knew of my existence, father and mother shipped me away to live with my grandparents in Gosha.” I turn my eyes towards the Duke and notice he is gazing lovingly at his son. He does have some family left after all.

“When I was around five years old, father came to us and told us what the King had done. Grandmother was distraught over the news. Her only daughter was locked within the walls of Castle Rae by a madman. It was from that day forth, even from that young age, that I trained day and night to become the man I am today."

"And I am proud of all you have accomplished. We didn't send him away, Sadie, because we didn't want him; we sent him away to protect him from my brother. Only the angels know what Roger would have done if he discovered that Zahlia and I had a child. I don't even want to think about it, to be honest." Stephan turns away from us to grab himself a drink. I didn't miss the single tear that slid down the side of his cheek before his face turned out of view. What horrible times this man has had to endure, all because of his wretched brother.

"I hope you're not angry with me that I kept this from you. Queen Sarah believed that the less you knew the better. It was our way of protecting you against Roger." He may have lied about where he came from, but I see why. If the King had found out that his brother's son was living in the castle, who knows what horrors he would have inflicted upon Joshua?

"But the letters? If you knew what the secret was this whole time, why give them to me?"

"I wanted you to know that the Duke wasn't coming for the throne, he was coming for my mother. I'm confused though as to why the Queen never told me that she had died. I searched every day looking for her." He says hanging his head in sorrow, while I reach out and place a caring hand upon his chest. I'm here my love...

“That’s because, my darling boy, she is not dead.” The Queen states from the entrance to the tent holding nothing but a battle axe in her right hand. “I believe she is trapped in a chamber below the dungeons, and it’s about time we got her out.”

14

"I had a feeling she was still alive. I could see it in your eyes when you said she was dead. I knew you were not speaking the truth." The Duke's eyes light up with excitement as Queen Sarah walks around the grand desk to hug her brother-in-law.

"Only you would ever know I was lying..." She wraps her arms around his neck and pulls him in close. By the way he responds, I believe it has been quite some time since anyone has ever held him like that.

As slow as a snail he raises his arms and wraps them around her waist. But not a second passes before he drops his arms again. "I'm sorry about Hayley too. I tried everything I could to keep her safe, but Roger knew who she was and what she would mean to you. It was his last hurrah to murder her, but we will not let him get away with it. Especially when we have him on our side." They both glance our way and a shiver runs down my spine. What do they mean by that? I glance up at my lover and wonder what great threat he will be to the king. What does my Joshua have that the King's loyal servants don't?

"I'm ready for it," Joshua announces proudly and although I want nothing more than to see the King pay, I just don't want Joshua to go anywhere near him. His blackened armour seems to shimmer as the fires reflect off the reinforced metal. He is a man built for the task at hand. Always ready and prepared to accept the next order that is given. Everyone within Castle Rae knows he is the best fighter they've got. They just don't realise that he has been working for the opposite side this entire time.

"Good, the men are rallying as we speak. It won't be long until we breach the walls of Castle Rae once more. This time though, we go in from below." The Queen's eyes sparkle knowingly as she gazes upon the map of Castle Rae that's laid out on the table in front of her.

"You'll use the tunnels?" I primarily ask Joshua but it's the Queen who responds.

"Yes, we will. And I would like you to lead one of the teams back into the castle." Her eyes flick towards me and for a second, my stomach drops. What did she just say? She wants me to go back in?

"Me?" I ask surprised.

"Yes. You have trekked those tunnels many, many times. That is why the Duke and I believe you are the right people for the job." She says with pride. Of course, she does. She made sure I know those tunnels inside out.

“Are you sure Your Majesty? What if I come across one of the King's men in the tunnels? I know little to no combat. Joshua has taught me some but not much.” I ramble on, knowing it's futile.

“You will be fine, my dear Sadie. You will be followed by the Duke's greatest warriors. By chance, if you do come into any sort of trouble, they will be right there to protect you.” The Queen comes around the grand desk to stand before me. She has changed out of her beautiful golden sundress and is now in her very own blackened armour. I wonder who helped get her dressed?

“But I ...” Why am I even questioning my Queen. We all know that no matter what I say or do, I am going into those tunnels whether I like it or not, because I will do whatever the Queen asks of me. That is who I am. Her loyal servant. “Please accept my apologies my Queen, of course, I will lead your armies. However, what am I to do when I reach the end?”

“You will lead the men from the breaker's room to the grand foyer where you will meet up with Joshua and his men. From there you will escort them down the hallways and into the Dungeons. Zahlia is kept in a cell beneath the first floor. To access it, I believe you'll need to find the hidden panel at the very end of the first corridor on the right. There is supposed to be a candelabra to the left of it. Pull it forward and that should reveal the hidden passageway. You will know where to go from there.”

"And what about the King?" He is the only thing not mentioned in the Queen's plan to save the Duchess.

"Leave him to me. Both of you just focus on finding my wife, your mother. My men will do the rest." Duke Stephan stands tall on the other side of the desk, looking like the fierce warrior we were led to believe he was.

"And you're sure this plan of yours will work?" I ask sceptically. It has been years since this man has stepped foot anywhere in Castle Rae other than the throne room. Does he really remember his way around?

"Absolutely." The Duke says confidently, and I shift my gaze over to the Queen. She too radiates confidence, and so shall I. I can do this. There is no one alive who knows the ins and outs of Castle Rae better than Joshua and me. We can do this or at least die trying.

"Then I'm in," I declare as I nod my head and take a deep breath to calm my wayward nerves. I can do this...

"Wonderful! The men you will be leading back into the castle will meet you by the hatch door at sundown. Until then, make the most of the free time you have left tonight. You're both dismissed." As the last word leaves his mouth the Duke looks directly at his son. Another child he knows so little of. A child he sent away at such a young age, to be raised far away from the castle and the talons of his treacherous brother. This must be hard sending him back in, knowing that he may die trying to save his mother.

"Your Grace," I curtsy and begin to back away as Joshua reaches out his hand to stop me.

“Sadie wait,” Joshua pulls me over to where he’s standing and takes both my hands in his. “Do you love me?” He asks, catching me completely off guard.

“Of course I do Joshua, what’s going on?” Alarmed by the unreadable expression on his face, I glance over at the desk and see the Duke and the Queen staring at us.

“Do you remember when I told you that I am yours forever? That you have my heart completely.” He says tucking a lock of hair behind my ear.

“Yes, we were taking a stroll in the meadows. It was my birthday.” I utter as the memory of the sun on my skin filters through my mind. We had managed to get a whole afternoon off alone. It was one of the rarest occasions. One I will cherish forever.

“My feelings for you are as real as the air we breathe. You are my night and my day. My reason for being. I understand that you are just short of being of age, but I would like nothing more than to marry you. Here and now, on this very day.” He raises my hands and lays them upon his chest. His heart is beating hard and fast under my fingertips as he stares deep into my eyes. I feel an abundance of love and affection pouring out of him. His words speak the truth, he wants me and only me.

“Joshua...” I say as tears begin to well up in my eyes. “I will but how...” I pause as Joshua looks over at his father. There is no priest alive who would allow a woman under the age of eighteen to marry. However, a man with a higher ranking than a priest can grant permission for those to wed outside of the normal bounds. I may be three months shy of the legal limitations, yet standing here before me, is one of the few men who is able to grant me this most precious gift.

“Father, would you do me the honours of making this woman my wife?” Joshua asks with anticipation. I get the feeling that he doesn’t ask his father for much. How could he have when he's been living in the castle with his uncle while his father has been in exile?

“I will do so proudly my son. If you may,” The Duke gestures to the open space in front of him. Joshua turns away from me with our fingers linked together and guides us over towards his father. We stop a few feet away and turn to look at each other. Joshua’s happiness is evident by the grand smile on his face. “We are here on this very night to join Sir Joshua Tailgate and fair lady Sadie Jaymes.” The duke raises his sword between us and asks us to place our hands upon it. “Swear you now, on this sacred blade, that there is no reason known to you that this union should not proceed.”

The Duke looks towards Joshua as he begins to speak, “I do swear.”

“And you Sadie? Is there any reason known to you why this partnership should not be made?” The Duke asks.

“There is none.” I smile with joy knowing that this man is about to be my husband forever. Who knows what the future has in store for us, but for right now, it’s just the two of us. The Duke lowers his blade and hands it to the Queen standing next to him. She is beaming with happiness over our union. I don't think I've ever seen her so happy...

"Do you Sir Joshua Tailgate as husband of fair lady Sadie Jaymes, pledge before the angels and these witnesses to be her protector and her defender? To honour her and sustain her, in sickness and in health, in fair and in foul, to cherish and forsake all others, so long as you both shall live?" The Duke barely has time to finish before Joshua opens his mouth.

"I will," He beams, and I almost want to launch forward and kiss him however, I must wait. It is now my turn. The Duke repeats the words spoken and I can't help but wish my mother were here to see this. I kept my promise mother, just like I said I would...

"Sadie?" The Duke looks at me confused and I realise I've missed my cue.

"Yes, my apologies. I will!" I state more loudly than intended. Joshua shakes his head as he sighs in relief. Did he really think I was going to say no?

"May I ask if there are any rings?" The Duke looks over at Joshua who just shakes his head. I didn't even think about those.

"Not right now, no."

"Oh wait," The Queen steps forward removing her own band from around her finger. "Here, take mine." Joshua is about to object, but the Queen cuts him off. "It was your grandmother's, she would want you to have it." At the mention of his grandmother, Joshua raises his arm and the Queen places the jewel-encrusted ring into his open palm.

"Thank you," he says before turning back around. He gazes down at the ring and it kills me to think that this was his grandmother's, the one he never got to meet. "Sadie," Joshua speaks softly as he raises my left hand and slides the ring onto my finger. "Please receive this ring and wear it as a symbol of my trust, my respect and my love for you."

"Are you kidding? I'm never taking it off," I mutter not realising I said it out loud. Joshua's smile grows even wider as the Queen chuckles beside the Duke. "Well, it's true," I state smiling as I step closer to my husband.

"The ceremony's not over yet," Joshua whispers as I reach up on my tippy toes trying to steal a kiss. He glances over at his father who just shrugs his shoulders.

"It is now," I state reaching up and pulling his face down to meet mine. The Duke and the Queen clap beside us but I barely hear it as I'm lost in the excitement of this moment. Joshua is my husband. My husband! He wraps his arms around me and lifts me off my feet. I begin to giggle with glee as he spins us around the room.

"Now you two, get out of here. You don't have much time left until sundown." The Duke states with sadness lingering in his voice. I feel his pride all around us and for what Joshua just asked of him and I am happy he was prepared to do it for us. If it wasn't for him, I would not be Sadie Tailgate, the wife of a knight. I would still be plain old me.

Joshua doesn't allow us time to say any goodbyes as he carries me over the threshold and out of the tent. Our happy moment sours quickly when we hear the grunts of pain coming from the medical tent and the Duke's words come rolling back in. We don't have much time left at all. A sad smile plays on Joshua's lips, and I know he's thinking exactly the same thing as me.

We have no idea what's going to happen once we step foot into the castle? Are we going to be able to get to the dungeons without being seen or are we going to be intercepted by the King's men and never make it? Who really knows but to be honest, right now, all I want to think about is Joshua.

15

"Can we go somewhere to be alone?" I ask while still bundled up in his arms. His lips are hot as he presses them against mine. His need is all I can feel, and I am more than ready to fulfil it for him.

"I know a place," Joshua nods as he places me on my feet and grabs my hand. He leads us away from the Duke's tent, heading somewhere off in the distance. The smell of smoke and ash fills my nose and I almost have to cough due to the thickness of it. I notice the cause being all the tents that were burnt by the King's flaming arrows earlier this evening. Who knew that such little weapons could make such a huge impact?

We weave around two more tents before Joshua leads us to one with his shield resting against it.

"Your father allocated you a tent?" I ask as we walk through the open flaps and into the confined space. Other than a cot on the righthand side, there is nothing else in here.

"Yes, he said we would need rest before the final siege." He begins to unbuckle the side of his armour and I'm suddenly nervous, standing frozen in the doorway. Why am I like this? My hands have begun to sweat so I link them together behind me and I can feel my heart fluttering and racing inside my rib cage. Get your act together Sadie, you've got this.

"So, he gave you a cot big enough for one?" I joke as a shiver of anticipation runs throughout my entire body. My breaths come quicker as Joshua pulls his armour over his head, revealing the chain mail underneath. It fits his figure perfectly, showcasing every ounce of his muscles. Without a second thought, he removes the metal and drops it on the floor beside the bed.

"He knew you were small." Joshua chuckles, as his lips break into a mischievous grin. He comes to stand directly in front of me, wearing only his armoured pants and his padded shirt. In all the years we have been together, not once have I ever seen what lies beyond that padded shirt. My mouth goes dry at the thought.

"Joshua..." My eyes move to the bed and for a moment I wish time would stop. Joshua feels my hesitance and tenderly lifts my chin, staring deep into my eyes.

"It's alright my love, we don't have to do anything if you don't want to. I'd be happy to just lie here and hold you until we have to leave." His eyes search mine as he places his other hand on my waist. This is why I love him... He's always so caring, so thoughtful, so noble. Always making sure everyone else is alright before taking care of himself. Now it's my turn.

"I want you, Joshua, I have for the longest time. Although, it became set in stone the day the King put his hands on me. I knew then that I no longer wanted to wait. I wanted to make my own choices and not be forced to do something I didn't want to do. I just wish all of this was over. I told the Queen I was ready to go back in but really, I'm not. I'm terrified." A single tear slides down the side of my cheek and Joshua moves his thumb to wipe it away.

"I am too. I don't want you anywhere near Castle Rae, but you and I both know there is no one else alive who knows those tunnels better than us. I believe in you my love, you've got this. Once you reach the grand foyer, I'll be by your side every step of the way. You'll be safe, I promise." He lowers his head, resting his forehead against mine as we breathe each other in.

"You shouldn't make such promises Joshua. Only the angels know what we are walking into." I shake my head, dropping my gaze and looking down between us. I don't know how to fight, let alone stand against an army. Joshua raises my chin once more and I see a new flame burning deep within his stunning grey eyes.

"You are going to make it out of this alive Sadie Tailgate. I can and will promise you that. I will let no man stand in my way of getting you out of there. Do you understand?" His voice is deadly serious, and I know he is speaking the truth.

Ignoring my inner turmoil, I raise my arms and wrap them around his neck, pulling him down to meet my lips. My passion knows no bounds as I pour all my love deep into our unbroken kiss. His hands travel down my body until they reach the backs of my thighs. In one swift move, he hoists me off the ground and walks us over to sit on the edge of the cot.

I raise my knee a little higher against him and my simple maid's uniform splits from the ground up, reaching all the way to my left hip. I can feel the cool breeze against my heated skin. Joshua shifts my black hair over my shoulder and begins to trail kisses along my collarbone towards my neck. I sit up a little straighter as a shiver runs down my spine towards the apex between my thighs. Butterflies begin to take flight deep within me, a foreign sensation I have never felt before.

My head slightly tilts back as Joshua's tongue massages a tender spot at the base of my neck. I'm about to place my hands on his shoulders when he quickly swipes them both in a firm grip and holds them tightly behind my back. My breasts push up against him and I throw my head back as the feeling intensifies.

Moans begin to leave my mouth as my body uncontrollably rocks my hips back and forth on his lap. My body feels like a cannonball wanting to explode. Like a ball of yarn that's wound too tight and needs to break free.

"You're ravishing my love," Joshua whispers close to my ear before he nips the inside of my neck. At his words, my body explodes into a million pieces and I feel like I'm flying high above the ground where nothing can touch me.

My body tumbles over the pulsing sensation driving deep within my abdomen, while Joshua continues to place sweet little kisses on the side of my neck as loud noises uncontrollably escape my mouth. "You are amazing, my love." He whispers again as the sensation subsides. Who knew our bodies could ever make us feel this way?

"I love you, Joshua, with all of my heart," I mumble while placing my forehead against his. My breath is laboured and I am panting, yet I cannot wait to feel that amazing feeling again.

"And I you, my darling wife, my Sadie," He leans in for a kiss and I follow suit. The taste of salty ale fills my mouth as our tongues clash together in a frantic movement to get closer. He lets go of my arms and tightens his grip on my arse as he hoists me higher up against him, and my hands find their way into his unruly hair. It's greasy to the touch but I don't care, I need more. He moves me to the side and pushes me back so I'm lying on the bed.

His hands travel to the hem of his shirt as I raise myself onto my elbows. Now, this is something I want to see. His chiselled abs are mounds of perfection. Lifting my right hand, I run my fingers down the left side of his stomach. Oh, he will be my undoing.

"You like what you see?" He asks, stilling my hand at the base of his stomach.

“Most definitely,” I whisper sucking in my bottom lip. He is so beautiful.

“Good, because it’s all yours,” He shifts himself down above my knees and slowly slides my dress up my body. It gets a little stuck as he moves it over my bottom and has to lift me to remove the rest. A wave of embarrassment washes over me and yet is quickly forgotten as I get another glimpse of his perfect torso. I can’t believe he is mine.

“Maybe I should have gotten undressed before I laid down,” I state, helping him wriggle the last of the maid’s uniform over my head. I’m completely bare and unsure of what to do as Joshua’s eyes rake over my entire body.

“It definitely would have helped,” He says with a happy gleam in his eye as he lowers me back down onto the bed. This is the first time in my entire life that someone other than my mother has seen me completely bare. Going by the look Joshua’s giving me though, I believe he likes what he sees.

Joshua quickly stands up and removes his armoured pants, throwing them on top of the pile he left earlier. They make a clinking sound as they clash together with the breastplate, I have no time to sneak a glance as Joshua climbs back onto the bed and positions himself above me.

“You are the most magnificent creature I have ever seen.” He whispers into my ear, sending shivers coursing through my veins. Joshua places a kiss in the crook of my neck as he slides my legs apart with his. My body begins to shake with anticipation as I lift my arms and wrap them around his neck.

"And I'm all yours," I pull his lips down upon mine as he slides his arm under my left leg and runs his hand up my thigh.

"Are you ready?" He asks and I nod my head "This might hurt for a moment." He whispers as he positions himself at my opening and drives himself in quickly. My whole body screams in pain as Joshua stills deep within me allowing me time to adjust to the feel of him. A groan sounds from within my throat as I close my eyes and wish the pain to go away.

I slightly loosen my grip around Joshua's neck as I try to relieve some of my discomfort. Joshua must have mistaken that as permission to move and slowly begins to thrust himself in and out of me.

He must be very well endowed as he fills me completely. Sliding in and out of my wetness at a regular pace, Joshua starts kissing the tender spot on the side of my neck once more. The pain subsides as the butterflies begin to make their glorious comeback.

Joshua lifts my leg a little higher, driving even deeper into my wetness. Little uncontrollable moans leave my mouth with every thrust. Sweat begins to line my brow as Joshua's breaths get heavier. The butterflies are swarming, desperately wanting to be set free and without a conscious thought, I release them. My cries of ecstasy fill the air at the same moment Joshua finds his own glorious release and then stills, sated and deep within me. His breathing is heavy, as is mine, like we've just run the full length of the meadows.

He releases my leg, allowing me to place it back on the bed as he lifts his head away from the crook of my neck, gazing down at me.

"You are truly exquisite Sadie Tailgate. Genuinely the most amazing woman I've ever seen, and I can't wait to spend the rest of my life with you." And just like a switch, I'm reminded of our task at hand. Our lives may be cut short today but at least we have right now. This moment. This time to be truly who we want to be without any care in the world.

"You are my world Joshua; I never want to spend a moment without you in it."

"And you never will." He leans forward sealing his words with a kiss. Who knows how much time we have left but I'll be damned if I miss a single second.

"How do you feel?" He asks resting his forehead against mine.

"Truly magnificent," I whisper, before sealing his mouth with a kiss once more.

16

My hair swings to the side in the late afternoon breeze. The Duke allocated me armour of my own and I now await the arrival of the guards that I am to lead through the tunnels. The hatch door has been propped open with a rock, and although I am already surrounded by many men, I'm told there is still more to come.

I said my goodbyes to Joshua moments ago, and my heart is breaking at the possibility of never seeing him again but I must set that thought aside if I am to successfully lead these men back into Castle Rae. I need a clear mind to remember the steps, although, I don't think I could forget them even if I tried.

I stand on the edge of the Fairwind forest gazing at the castle not too far in the distance. Its high brick walls with the King's flag flying higher than the tallest keep loom over the vast space. I never would have realised just how big the castle is if I'd remained within the confines of those walls.

“Are you ready my child?” The Duke kindly asks over my shoulder. I half turn to look at him before returning my gaze to Castle Rae as he comes to stand by my side.

“I’m not so sure Your Grace. I’m afraid my feelings are a little conflicted.”

“And you have every right to be. This is a big task the Queen and I have requested of you. However, I will have you know, that I have put my best men in your brigade. You need not worry; I have warned them to make it their life’s mission to make sure you’re safe.” The Duke and I stare far into the distance. I know what today means for him. He may end this day as king with his lover in tow, or he will crash and burn with myself along with him. Only time will tell.

“Thank you, Your Grace. I will do my very best.”

“That I know you will. Your team has assembled. Joshua has already begun his descent, but you may begin whenever you’re ready. Take your time and remember the steps. I believe in you. We all believe in you.” Without another word he turns and walks back to the tents camped out in the middle of the meadow. There are so many men surrounding me, waiting for me to lead them through the tunnels and into chaos. My heart is beating at a million miles a second and although I’m struggling to breathe, I walk over to the hatch door.

There is a massive rock that stands around waist height not far from the entrance and I decide to make my announcement from atop it. With the help from a nearby soldier, I am hoisted upon it.

"Please listen..." I yell, hoping all of those around me can hear. "I have manoeuvred these tunnels many times over. There is little to no visibility, and it is recommended that we crawl through on our hands and knees but I understand that time is of the essence so instead we will attempt crouching to try and move through them quicker.

We are not able to use lamps or fires and talking is to be strictly no talking. You are going to have to hold on to the person in front of you to be able to determine the way forward. Is that understood and do you have any questions?" Looking at the blank expressions staring back at me, I continue. "It's going to take us quite a while a long time to get through these tunnels so let's begin. Form a line behind me and let's go." I jump down from the rock and take a deep breath.

"You've got this," I whisper to myself as a soldier grabs ahold of my armour plate at the back. I look over my shoulder and see a clear line of men ready to follow me into the unknown. Stepping forward I feel the mass move with me and lower myself into the hatch.

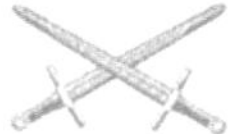

It's cold and dark and the smell of damp wood fills my nose as I round yet another corner. The shuffling of feet is all I've heard for hours as we've manoeuvred these ridiculously low walkways. If only the Queen had the foresight to make them just a little bit higher, then we wouldn't have to be crouching and my legs wouldn't be burning. Only a little bit further. Twenty-six... Twenty-seven... Feeling around on my right, I feel the corner and move around it. I feel the tug behind me as the men follow me through yet another change of direction. Seventeen... Eighteen... Again, on the right and follow through. Just two more corners.

I hear chatter coming through the walls and slow my pace just a smidge. My heart picks up a little as I hear the voices getting closer to the wall beside me. The soldier behind me tugs on my armour, beckoning me to stop. My breath gets caught in my throat. They are close enough now that we can make out every word they are saying.

"What are they waiting for? It's been hours since the attack in the throne room and now it's like they're teasing us! Begging us to come outside and strike first. If only the King would allow us to step foot beyond these walls. I'm itching to make those dirty bastards bleed."

"Calm down Rutherford. You will get your chance, trust me. They won't stay out there forever. Not when we have something they want."

"But the Bitch told him she's dead!" The one closest to the wall replies angrily.

"He's not after her you idiot. Well not anymore. He wants the crown. Now get off your arse and let's go. We have to patrol the east wing before the King comes back." The King's gone? Where'd he go?

Hearing the voices fade away I begin to move the brigade once more. Right around the next corner, one... two... There is only one more corner to go and I feel like I'm about to be sick. I have been psyching myself up for hours to get to this moment. Twenty-Six... Twenty-Seven... Left.

Only fourteen steps away from me and what lies beyond the wardrobe doors. Will there be horrors that I don't even want to think about, or will there be nothing at all? I close my eyes and take a deep breath as I think back to the peaceful moments Joshua and I shared just hours ago. Especially those of his lips on my neck, and my legs wrapped around his back. I know this is not the time to be thinking of this but if I'm about to die, I want that moment to be the last thing I see.

The slab of wood still blocks the doorway, so I remove it and place it on the ground beside me. I feel the anxiety radiating off the men behind me and know they too are wondering what's beyond the door. Feeling around on the righthand side, I find the tiny little pull string which opens the flap and yet, I hesitate.

I know I don't want to go out there, but these men are depending on me to get them to the grand foyer, so I pull the string and the door swings inwards.

Pushing the cloaks out of the way I move to the side and allow the first few men to climb out in front of me. The room appears to be vacant as I get to my feet. My legs are stiff and ache in so many places and my back hurts from being hunched over for so long.

The room is filling up quite fast as all the men file out of the narrow passageway. With almost no breathing room left, I squeeze my way over to the men crowded by the door leading out into the castle.

"Would you mind checking the hallways, please? I think it's time we move on." I whisper quietly, not wanting to alert anyone who may be beyond the door. Without a word the two men closest nod their heads. They turn the knob ever so slightly and pull it so it's slightly ajar. One of them sticks their head out and checks around. For a moment there, I hold my breath.

"All clear," He says pulling his head back in and swings the door wide open. Everyone begins to file out with their swords drawn, everyone except me that is. The Duke did give me a sword, although I have no idea how to use it. When Joshua trained me all those months ago, I only ever learnt how to use a dagger. He believed that if someone was going to attack me, a dagger would be way more useful than a sword. That is why Joshua stashed a fine little blade in my boot when I said goodbye to him this evening. He is always thinking one step ahead.

"To the left!" I whisper as loudly as I dare, hoping everyone around me can hear. As one, the group collectively moves and begins to travel down the hallway. I'm in the middle of the pack, near the front but not close enough to get in harm's way. The Duke wasn't lying when he said these men would protect me.

The hallways are quiet as we make our way down the stairs to the second landing. It's dark, as no torches have been lit, but thankfully, I know the way.

We reach the Queen's chambers without incident and although I'm grateful, it still feels wrong. Where are they all? The King wouldn't be keeping them away without reason. The hallways should be flooded with men. This isn't right. It feels like a trap!

"We need to go left," I whisper again, and the group moves quickly around the corner.

"FIRE!!" A person around the bend yells and I drop to the floor as I hear arrows fly overhead. Grunts from the men standing around me echo in my ears as they fall to the floor beside me. Their blood spills out all over the ground while the sound of swords clashing together fills the air. My ears are ringing as I reach for my sword. I may not know how to use it, but I think it's best to have it out regardless.

I rise to my feet and follow the rushing crowd. They are heading towards the fray not away from it and so shall I. I need to make it to the grand foyer, to Joshua. I hold onto the back of someone's armour and charge with my head down. I don't want to witness the violence that is unfolding around me, however, I know I will eventually. I step over a soldier lying dead on the floor and realise it's time.

Raising my head, I see a swarm of the Kings guards blocking the way. We really need to get past them. There is no other way to get to the foyer from where we are standing. Taking a deep breath, I look for my target and charge forward with my weapon drawn. The King's guard is distracted by two of the Duke's men and hopefully won't see me coming. I'm less than four feet away when he turns around and we lock eyes.

The sneer that crosses his face is only there momentarily as I plunge my blade deep into his abdomen, right below his breastplate. It makes the most unusual sound as I withdraw my sword and head towards another man standing a little to my right. The Duke's guard catches his attention just as I get close enough to sink my blade into his back. I try to pull it out, but it doesn't move. Raising my leg, I kick the King's guard out of the way, setting my blade free.

A stinging sensation tingles in my right calf, making me look down. I've been nicked by a swinging blade. Blood begins to drip down into my boot but I must pay it no notice. We need to keep moving. The Duke is coming in after Joshua and me to find his brother and kill him. We need to make sure there is a clear path, so he has the chance to do so.

"Keep moving! Push the bastards back!" One of the soldiers asserts from somewhere within the pack and it's as if they are a swarm of bees. I feel the force as they all begin to push forward, and we manage to make ground.

I stand motionless in the middle of the battle, not knowing whether to keep going or stay and fight. The pain in my calf is intensifying and I'm afraid to look at it. I can't tell how deep it is and I'm not really sure I want to know. It must be bad though as I feel the blood continuously sliding down my leg.

"Ma'am we need to keep moving." A soldier says next to me, but I don't move. He stares at me as if I've lost my mind. Maybe I have as this really isn't the time or place to be having such a moment. "Sadie!" The soldier yells this time grabbing my attention and it's only now that I realise it's Kyle, Princess Hayley's guard.

"You switched sides?" I ask surprised as I look upon a friendly face. I'm so thankful he is on our side. I would hate it if we had to take him down for standing in our way.

"Did you really think I'd stay with him after what he did to Hayley?" He looks at me sceptically as a sad expression dulls his handsome face.

"No, of course not," I say shaking my head. Kyle protected the Princess for years only to hand her over to her killer. Although no one would have thought that the King would have done such a thing, especially to his own niece. "I'm so glad to see you though."

"And I'm happy to see you too but we really need to keep moving." He says as he's about to walk away but I still can't move.

"My leg." Kyle looks down and sees the open gash. Without a word, he tears some fabric away from his padded shirt and ties it around the wound. I scream out in agony as the pressure is applied and a different sort of pain ignites from my injury.

“Hopefully that will help, can you walk?” He asks as he stands up to his full height. The fighting seems to have moved on down the hall and I know it's time to go.

“I’ll manage, thank you.” I test my footing and although it hurts badly, I know with adrenaline on my side, I’ll make it through this. “Let’s go,” I say and make my way towards the men fighting at the end of the hall. I may have a severely bad limp, but I will not let that stop me.

We are not far away from the grand foyer now, and I feel with every man we take down, it gets us that one step closer to achieving what we set out to do.

17

Hundreds of men crowd the space that is the grand foyer. Swords clash as arrows wiz from the left to the right. Who knows how long Joshua and his team have been down there fighting alone? My men rush down the stairs after defeating their fray to join the others. Soon the entire room is almost completely overrun by the Duke's men.

I stand at the top of the stairs not wishing to go any further. My eyes scan my surroundings for a familiar face, however I don't see him. Where is he? Grunts and screams filter up from below and my heart aches with nervousness. I need to see him.

My leg burns a new sort of pain as I take one step down onto the stone steps. Gritting my teeth, I fight against the pain and fear to see over the balustrade and down into the fray below. I witness the exact moment a King's guard is decapitated and I almost pass out from the sight. There is so much blood. I move another step down but this time I cannot contain my anguish and let out a pain filled scream of my own. It rings in my ears as I tighten my grip on the stone banister.

“SADIE!” Joshua bellows from somewhere within the battle below and my head whips up. He’s alive! Filled with new determination, I manage to ignore the pain travelling through me and almost sprint down the stairs towards where the voice came from.

“JOSHUA!” I scream and he returns my call. I track the sound of his voice and find him over near the double doors. The only problem being the wall of men standing between us. Gripping my sword tight I swing it around, hoping to hit as many of the King’s guards as I can as I fight my way over to the man I love. I see a lot of the King’s armour standing in my way, so I just keep swinging. I feel my blade slice through a man on my left. It's not enough to take him down permanently but it is enough to momentarily distract him so someone else can.

“SADIE!!” Joshua calls again. His voice so close that I feel as if I could reach out and touch him. A man falls to the ground in front of me and there he is. My Knight in shining armour, which at this moment in time is completely covered in blood.

“Joshua.” I almost weep as I stumble forward and into his arms. The moment my body connects with his, he moves us out of the foyer and into the courtyard, away from the fight. I know that he should stay, in there but right now I need him more.

"You're hurt." He says concerned, as he pulls back and drops down on one knee. "You need a fresh bandage. This one is soaked." He pulls up the base of his armour and he too rips a piece of fabric away. Do all the guards do this when someone is hurt? With feather-light touches, Joshua removes the tourniquet that's wrapped around my leg and places the new sash over the open wound. "How did this happen? You were supposed to be kept away from the fight." I hear the frustration lingering in his voice but I pay it no attention.

"I was trying to be brave," I say courageously as Joshua stands up next to me. His normally shaggy hair is wet and dripping with sweat. He clenches his jaw and I can feel his annoyance over my injury. We knew something like this was going to happen though. I'm just thankful it wasn't any worse.

"I have no doubt you were my love, but please next time, just leave it to those who have been trained to fight."

Like I had a choice, but I can understand his concern. "I'll try," I whisper as he leans forward and places a sweet kiss on my lips. I drape my arms around his neck holding him close, while he wraps his arms around my back. I've been so afraid and to have him in my arms feels like heaven. "I was so scared," I whisper finally, allowing myself to breathe.

"I know, my love. Me too..." he says as he pulls me closer and kisses me more passionately than before. "You did great. I'm so incredibly proud of you. Just one more task and then we are done." I nod my head, not wanting to say any more. "I spoke with my father before we left and he believes with all the commotion going on up here, we will only need a small team to go into the dungeons with us. They have already assembled by the gates. They are just waiting for us. But if you feel like you can no longer continue, I completely understand."

"The Queen asked me to complete this task. Wounded or not. I'm going to see it through." I go to step forward and almost stumble from the pain that shoots up my leg. Joshua reaches forward and places his arm under my own to help support the weight on my leg as we make our way back into the foyer.

"You sur are stubborn. The Duke should be here soon anyway with his brigade. Hopefully, he'll be able to disable the King before we return." Joshua's grey eyes turn darker as he glances towards the west wing where the King resides. I wouldn't be surprised if he has locked himself away in his chambers waiting for his men to do his bidding for him. He is not the kind of man who likes getting his fingers dirty, especially when he has a band of miscreants to do it for him.

"I do not doubt that he shall. Your father is an especially determined man. Even more so now that he believes your mother may still be here, locked up in the dungeons."

"How right you are." We pass a few men fighting their way closer to us, but the Duke's soldiers fend them off. With those in the foyer distracted, we manage to slip out the back and away from the fight.

It's a short walk from the entrance to the rear of the castle, everyone knows that the castle is taller rather than wider or spread out. The Tailgate's ancestors wanted to provide a show of strength to competing forces by building the tallest fortress in all of the regions. Little did they know that symbol of strength and their wealth would one day land in the hands of a greedy, backstabbing tyrant who cares for nothing but himself. All of that is about to change.

Roughly ten men crowd around the entrance to the dungeons, and I'm overjoyed to see that Kyle is among them.

"Alright gentlemen, gear up, let's go." Joshua pulls me closer, getting ready to stay behind with me but I object. They need him on the front line.

"You go first, I'll stay at the back with Kyle. Trust me, he will protect me." I pull his arm away from my waist and although he tries to say no, I don't let him. "They need you more, now go." I push him away as I lean towards Kyle. He takes my arm and rests it over his shoulder, keeping the weight off my leg. I lean slightly forward and withdraw my small dagger hidden within my boot. It may not be large, but I will definitely be able to handle it more precisely than a sword.

"Here we go," I say quietly as we follow the group of men down the stairs and into the darkness below.

18

The air is stale and damp and sweat clings to my upper brow. I could never have imagined the dungeons were so far beneath the castle's main landing. We have been walking down for what feels like a lifetime.

"Up ahead," Joshua whispers loudly so the whole convoy can hear. I peer over the soldier's heads and see a fire flickering not too far beneath our feet. I hear someone coughing below and it only dawns on me now that there would be other souls down here and not just the Duchess. Of course there is, how could I be so naive?

We reach the bottom step as the cells come into view. Hands reach toward us through the iron bars and although I want nothing more than to help them, they must wait. We need to find out why they are down here first and that will have to come at another time.

"Fan out," Joshua commands as he stays close to my side. He looks over at Kyle and nods his head towards a corridor in front of us as if to say search down there. Kyle reluctantly removes his arm from around my waist and heads off in the direction he was ordered to. Joshua stands no more than three feet away but for some weird reason, it feels like there is a whole meadow between us.

The air is thick in my throat, and I have to cough away the ickiness of it. There is a slight breeze coming from the landing at the top of the stairs and it pains me to think about when these people last saw sunlight. The conditions these poor souls are in is depressing but I know they mostly likely have done something criminal or even treacherous but still. The smell of human despair and defecation cannot be missed.

I glance down the way the Queen told me to go and not a single fire light is lit. All the other torches are burning brightly but not that corridor. It's as dark as the blackest night. I hear the soldiers making their return by their approaching footsteps. I guess we are...

"I knew I'd find you here. You never could leave poor Joshua alone now, could you? You're such a stupid girl for thinking he'd ever be interested in you." Lance sneer's quietly in my ear as his grip tightens over my mouth, his other arm wrapping around my waist pulling me flush against him. The smell of days-old whisky is ever present on his breath. I smelt it on him the last time we encountered each other.

I begin to writhe in his grasp, but he will not give. Instead of making a show of his presence, he begins pulling me back the way we came. I did not come this far to let this man take control over me. With my hands still free, I flip my dagger around in my hand and plunge the blade deep into Lance's upper thigh. His scream of pain fills the room and Joshua whirls around in surprise.

I remove my blade as Lance pushes me away. I stumble forward onto the floor as Joshua races past me. With his sword raised high I know for sure he will reach his mark. The squelch of Joshua's blade piercing Lance's skin is deafening in the suddenly now quiet room. A shiver runs down my spine from the noise. After all of this is over, I never wish to be included in such matters ever again.

After deeming his component dead, Joshua rushes to my side.

"I'm fine, he only caught me off guard. That is all." I rest my hand on the side of his worried face, but it does nothing to mend his concerns.

"Are you..." He begins but I cut him off. We need to move.

"I'm fine, we need to keep searching. I need the torches lit down the right corridor if you please. We need to find your mother." I whisper the last part quietly and Joshua's eyes light up just a smidge. It has been many years since he laid eyes upon her. I do hope she recognises him. That's if she truly is down there.

The soldiers get to work lighting the way as I make it to my feet. Feeling a little more at ease with my wound, I continue on my way with no help from the men around me.

Joshua stands guard on my left as the others fan out around us. Sliding my blade back into my boot, I see the candelabra at the end of the corridor and limp over.

The Queen mentioned that the hidden panel should be on the right, although I see nothing but bricks. Joshua and I glance at each other as I grasp the candle stick and pull it forward. I stare at the brickwork beside me, but nothing happens.

"I did it right, didn't ..." I begin to say just as there is a great big whoosh, and a gust of air shoots out in my face. A hidden door appears exactly where the Queen said it would.

I hear Joshua murmuring something to the men behind us, but I pay no notice. There are voices filtering up from below and I know that there is someone else down there with the Duchess.

"Joshua," I say with concern lingering in my voice. He stops his conversation behind me and comes to my side as quick as lightning.

"What is it?" He asks but then he hears them too. One voice, in particular, and his eyes go wide as he too recognises who it is. Without another thought, I grab his hand and pull him down the stairs behind me. My leg throbs in protest but I do not care. If the Duchess is really down there, we must save her.

The hatch door slides shut behind us, enclosing us in darkness. For a moment I want to hesitate, but I know we can't. The voices are getting louder the further we descend and as we reach the bottom step, we witness the Duchess getting slapped hard across the face. Joshua leaves my side and takes a few steps ahead of me.

"Lay your hands on my mother again and it will be the last thing you ever do," Joshua snarls at the King on the opposite side of the room. I'm shocked by the nature of these chambers. It is not what I pictured at all going by the conditions the men and women are forced to endure upstairs. This room is fit for a Queen. It is almost an exact replica of Queen Sarah's chambers in the east wing.

A wooden four-poster bed sits in the middle of the room. Lavish, golden silks hang from post to post. A dresser the size of a grand table sits on the left-hand side and a wardrobe fit for her title sits on the other. There are books and lounge chairs scattered around the room, proving evident that she has been down here for quite some time.

"Mother?" The King asks in complete disbelief as he gazes upon my husband and then back at the woman standing no more than three feet away from him. Her brown hair falls in big curls down her back as her night dress hangs loosely from her body. Her eyes are trained on the young man standing before me and it's as if she too doesn't believe who she is seeing.

"Joshua?" She asks cautiously as he slightly nods his head. At the acceptance of his name the Duchess begins to weep. "Oh, my sweet boy... Never in this lifetime did I ever believe that I would see you again. I have missed you terribly..." Her tears begin to stream down her face as the

King standing beside her straightens his back. His face contorts into something vile as he looks over at us.

"I always knew something was off about you, boy. You never could conform like the rest of them. Maybe it's about time I taught you the true meaning of being a King." He reaches into his coat pocket and produces a tiny little device. Placing it to his lips he emits a high pitch chime which makes me cover my ears. What in the realm is that? The noise didn't affect Joshua in the slightest, so I'm guessing he has heard it before. The King stands proudly on the other side of the room, gazing expectantly at the stairwell we came out of.

"There's no one around to save you, Your Majesty. Not even Lance who I bet you placed outside this door, for this particular moment. I'll have you know though that I took good care of him a short while ago." The King raises his brow in surprise, he was not expecting that. And of course, he wasn't. I bet Lance was supposed to be his saving grace. Now, what is he going to do?

"It seems you've managed to take me by surprise boy. Now it's my turn." A sickening sneer breaks out on his face as a small dagger slides down into the palm of his hand from somewhere hidden within his coat. My eyes go wide and it feels like I'm witnessing deja vu as the King turns towards the Duchess. Oh, not again...

"No," Is the only word I manage as Joshua launches himself forward. The King places his hand around Zahlia's throat as he raises the dagger towards her face. Joshua's steps are gigantic as he sprints over and rips the King away from his mother. Joshua throws him up against a wall before withdrawing his sword from its sheath. A brass key bounces out of the King's coat pocket stopping just short of the Duchess's right foot.

"Sadie, take my mother and go. I'll handle this." My heart stops at his command. I know he's asking me to leave to protect me, but he's seriously gone mad if he believes I'm going to leave him alone with this deranged killer.

"But Joshua..." I begin to plead but he cuts me off.

"GO! NOW!" He almost growls while never taking his eyes off the King who is rising to his feet. The Duchess heeds the warning in her son's voice, she swipes the brass key from the floor and dashes in my direction. She grabs my forearm and begins to drag me back towards the stairs as the men begin to circle each other.

We hit the bottom step and I turn around. I don't want to witness the fight that's about to take place and my heart breaks at the thought of leaving Joshua behind.

My leg burns as we race up the stairs. It gets darker the further we ascend, and I have no idea how we are ever going to find our way out. We reach the hidden door and I begin to bang my fists against it. Swords clash together behind me, and my mood really takes a nosedive. Tears for what might occur stream down my face, and I desperately wish for all of this to be over. There can only be one outcome from the fight happening behind me and I pray my Joshua is victorious.

“Where is it?” Zahlia whispers beside me as I hear her dragging the brass key along the wall. What is she doing? I begin to wonder but then I hear her. “Got it.” She sighs in relief as the door clicks and slides open. A breeze of stale air hits us as we open the door, leading out into the dungeon corridors and I almost gag again. She goes to withdraw the key but I stop her.

“Joshua will not be able to get back out after he wins if you take the key,” I mutter quickly.

“And if he doesn’t? I do not want that monster walking the halls searching for me once more. I’m done with him and this place.”

“Then it’s best we find your husband and tell him where his brother is before it’s too late.” There is a loud grunt behind us, and I suddenly realise I need to get her Grace out of here. My sole purpose now is to keep her safe.

“Stephan?” She whispers and her face lights up with hope.

“Yes, and I believe he is upstairs now looking for the King. If we hurry, we can save Joshua and end all this madness.” Pulling her hand away from the key, I lead her up the corridor towards the staircase. We see no one but those enclosed behind the bars as we go, and I begin to wonder what happened to our team. I doubt they would have just left.

We ascend the stairs quickly, making it to the top landing in record time. My leg protests at the quickened pace, but I don’t stop. Joshua needs our help.

The grand foyer is empty when we walk in, and I notice that the fight seems to have moved outside into the courtyard. The high walls looming over all who those who are battling within the vast space. There would have to be over a hundred men and women fighting down there. Fighting for our freedom.

I see the Duke fighting not too far from where we are standing and decide we can make it. Withdrawing the blade from my boot, I hold it close as we weave our way through the throngs of people killing each other all around us.

Forgoing formalities, I believe the best way to capture the Duke's attention would be by calling out his first name, so I do. "STEPHAN!" I yell and as quick as lightning he turns his face towards me. He swings his eyes back to his opponent, raises his sword and hits the young lad on the head with the butt of his blade. The kid falls to the ground unconscious.

He pushes soldiers out of the way as he makes his way over. He looks at me pleadingly, but I'm not sure of the question he is asking. It isn't until he gets much closer that I realise he has yet to see the Duchess and he all but collapses as he finally views his wife as she steps up beside me.

The Duchess says nothing as she barges past me, straight into her lover's arms. He holds her closely, while he kisses her passionately. Only the angels truly know how long it's been. I feel for them deeply however, another pressing matter needs our attention. My husband is currently fighting the King of Castle Rae with no backup on the way. He needs help now.

As the lovers rest their foreheads against each other I wish for nothing more than to give them a moment, but time is of the essence.

"Your Grace, sorry for the intrusion but Joshua is still down in the dungeons battling the King. He caught us off guard as we believed him to be in the west wing. We need to send back up as soon as..."

"THE KING IS DEAD!" Joshua shouts from the open doorway, holding up the King's severed head as proof. Everyone around us stops dead in their tracks as they all turn to see what happened. He did it! He really did it.

Zahlia sighs heavily behind me and I know she is relieved, she no longer has to worry about the King.

"All hail King Joshua!" The Duke yells behind me and all of those around take a knee. Oh, my word, that's right. You kill the King; you automatically take the throne. I fall to my knee as well, realising that what we have together, can now never be. He is now the King; the people of Castle Rae will not accept a maid for their Queen. It's strictly not done.

My heart breaks at the thought of never being with him again but know it's the way it will have to be.

"You may rise," Joshua says a little awkwardly before everyone gets to their feet. A soldier from the Duke's brigade walks forward and introduces himself before relieving Joshua of the King's severed head. Joshua flicks away some of the remaining blood from his fingers before peering out into the crowd.

He may not know how to rule a kingdom, but he has already won the people's hearts. He managed to do that a long time ago. That was why the King appointed him the high Knight of Castle Rae. He knew exactly how to deal with people and oversee any situation thrown his way. That is why he will be a fantastic King, I just won't be standing by his side, not this time.

19

My chambers are dark and gloomy when I finally return to them just before dawn. My armour is splattered with blood, and I make quick work removing it from my body.

I ducked out of the courtyard moments after Joshua was announced as the new King. I didn't want to wait around for him to find me. The next conversation we are going to have is going to be hard enough and I wish to not have it after such an ordeal.

Water still remains in the wash basin, so I grab a cloth and begin to scrub the night's nastiness off of my body. I'm scrubbing so hard; it feels like I'm washing a layer of skin off. My arms burn as I continue to scrub and I fear I will never be able to wash away the memories from this evening.

Tears fall steadily down my cheeks for I no longer know what to do with my life. The dream was to leave this place with Joshua by my side but all of that has changed. With the King dead, the Queen no longer holds rank, and I will return to being an ordinary scullery maid. Working for who, I do not know.

I still have the choice to leave Castle Rae when I turn eighteen but where would I go? With no coin or title to my name, it is best that I just stay here and live my life as if nothing has happened. But how am I to do that when I'll see Joshua every single day for the rest of my life?

I drop the washcloth into the basin and cry heavy tears as my heart breaks even further. I want to curl up and let a huge hole swallow me up. I feel empty, hollow even. Is this how widows feel after losing their loved ones to battle? But I didn't lose mine to war, well actually now that I think about it, I did. The war with the King inevitably took my husband away from me.

His greed for power is what caused all of this in the first place, and his lust for things that were not his. I cannot begin to fathom the things the Duchess had to endure while trapped below the castle all these years. He may have only threatened me, but I fear he did way worse to her.

Her letters come to mind, and I peer over at the nightstand. There are still two letters I'm yet to read and without another thought, I walk over and pick the first one up. Placing it on my lap, I swipe a match and light the candle stick that's sitting beside me.

Lifting the worn paper, I carefully unfold it and begin to read...

My Dearest Stephan

I have news. Your brother has found himself a suiter. Although I am relieved, as this means we will not wed, he has decided that I will still not be allowed to leave. He is infatuated with me my love and it sickens me to my core every time he tries to touch me.

Please save me from this madness and come home.

I miss you terribly.

Yours truly

Z

After placing it back on the table, I grab the other one.

My Dearest Stephan

This is my last letter as the King has instructed me to never write to you again. He told me to say goodbye as I will from this day forth be his property and never step foot outside of Castle Rae again.

It pains me to say this to you now, but I am with child my love. A moving, kicking little bundle of joy. A perfect little reminder that I will always have a piece of you here with me.

I love you my darling, Stephan. I will for the rest of my days.

Until the day we can be together again.

Yours truly.

Z

There is a slight rap on my door, and I quickly pull my head away from the last letter. If only the Duke knew that his wife was with child, I doubt he would have ever left in the first place. The person knocks again but this time louder.

"One moment," I say before rushing over to the dresser and pulling out a nightgown. I slip it over my head before walking to the door. I know who's there before I even open it. The hairs on the back of my neck stand on edge as I slightly open the door. "Your Majesty?" I mutter as I awkwardly curtsey in front of him.

"Please don't call me that." He whispers before pushing the door open just enough for him to squeeze through. I'm about to object but get a glimpse of his face and stop. He appears horrified and I don't blame him. It's not only my life that has changed on this day, but his too.

"Are you alright?" I ask as I close the door behind him.

"Does it look like I'm alright Sadie?" He mutters a little disheartened.

"Honestly, no. You look like death." I walk over to the basin and tip the used water into the bucket on the floor. I grab the jug from beside the bed and fill up the basin before retrieving a clean cloth from the top of my dresser. "Please sit," I say softly, gesturing towards the bed. The cot groans under the weight of Joshua in his armour. I ring out the sodden washcloth and walk over to him.

His eyes are trained on my face, they never waver as I close the gap between us. They appear sad and yet also hopeful. Today was a horrible day for him. He may have saved his mother from the depths of Castle Rae, but he also lost his sister. He always told me how much he despised her; in honesty we all did. She did not act like the Princess she was led to believe she was. Now that I think about it though, maybe she knew all along that she wasn't the heir. Maybe the King had mentioned something to her, but we will never know.

I raise his chin a little higher and begin to clean the deep gash on his forehead. He closes his eyes and sighs. For someone I have no issues talking to, I'm finding it hard to speak. The latest revelation has completely thrown me out of balance. I no longer know what to say or how to say it, or how to act in front of him. I'm overwhelmed and confused.

"Please don't cry," He whispers pulling my hand away from his face and opening his eyes. I didn't even realise I was until he mentioned it. The water gates completely open within me and I fall to my knees in front of him. Since the moment the "King" entered my quarters, I've been holding myself back, trying to bury the pain and the heartache.

My sobs are loud and out of control as they rack my body. I hear Joshua move around above me, but I can't look. He is my King, my KING! He should not see a maid act this way. I should not have let myself get like this; and in all honesty, I should have known better than to open my door when in such a matter. I truly am a fool for loving a Knight. I should have known back when we began that this would never work.

Joshua scoops me up and places me on his lap, cradling my head against his chest. His armour is gone and only his padded shirt remains. He holds me for as long as I need and although I know I shouldn't, I let him. He smells of sweat mixed with metal. The kind of scent that makes me feel safe. Like no matter what comes my way, he will always protect me.

"Joshua..." I begin pulling my head away from his chest. "We can't do this anymore. You can't be here." I climb off his lap as he gazes at me confused. Not wanting to see his eyes, I turn around and head back over to the basin. I place the washcloth in the water and ring it out as I draw in all the courage I have left to say what needs to be said. "A King does not come down to these quarters. He marries beautiful Princesses or Duchesses from neighbouring kingdoms. He does not marry maids.

The people of Castle Rae will shame you for being with such a lower class and I will not allow that Your Majesty. I do not want them to hate you before your reign even begins." My voice breaks as I say those words and yet they are true. People will judge him, and although our people are kind, there are still rules in place. Rules that I wish weren't there, but they are, and I cannot change that.

"Sadie..." He gets to his feet and walks over to stand behind me. "Please look at me," he whispers and even though I know I will probably cry, I obey. His eyes are searching mine as he reaches forward and takes both my hands in his. "All that you said is true, however, you are no longer lower class. You are my wife, a lady of Castle Rae. The people will love you. You helped save Castle Rae from under the reign of an evil man. You helped save us all, Sadie."

"But I did only what was requested of me, Joshua. Nothing more."

"If it wasn't for you, those men wouldn't have made it inside these walls. We would have been caught off guard by Lance and never would have survived to find the hidden door. So, you may think you did nothing but in reality, you did everything."

"But I'm just a maid Joshua. I know no life outside of my duties."

"You are more than you know, Sadie." I shake my head in denial and avert my gaze. Even if I am a lady by marriage, I still don't believe the people would accept me. "Sadie..." He tilts my chin, so I am forced to look up at him. "You need to understand, I live and breathe for you... Everything that just happened, I did it for you, for us... You are and will always be my Queen Sadie Tailgate. Nothing will ever change that. You don't need a title or rank for me to love you the way I do. You just need to be you."

"You did it for me?" I ask sceptically.

"Yes, however saving my mother was for me, but killing the King; that was for you. He should never have laid his hands upon you." His eyes turn dark as he mentions the Kings transgressions. That day is repeated frequently in my mind. It is most certainly going to take me some time to forget. Silence falls between us and only the angels know what he is thinking.

"What do we do now?" I ask.

"I don't know. But whatever it is, we will do it together." Joshua pulls me close and lays a sweet kiss upon my lips and the moment we connect, I know that as long as we are together everything will be alright. His words are spoken with so much confidence that I have no choice but to agree. My whole body relaxes as I look up into the eyes of the man I love. The man who owns my heart completely and will never allow anything to happen to me.

Although I am still a little concerned about the backlash from our people, he is not. And that is enough for me. He loves me with all his heart and I am happy to say I feel the same.

"Together," I repeat his word and place my head against his chest. My face breaks into the biggest smile as all my dreams are coming true. I feel his happiness too as he leans back and captures my lips, kissing me until the sun comes up. He is my Knight, my King, and forever from this day forth, my husband.

THE END.

Acknowledgements

Firstly, I would like to say a huge thank you to my Husband Robby. You encourage me every day to follow my dreams and you were my inspiration behind Revelations. I just hope that one day you will actually read it.

Secondly, I would like to thank my mother and nanna for helping me come up with a title for my love story. I'm a sucker for one worded titles.

A big thank you to Gregg for being my guanine pig and reading my book before anyone else. I really appreciate it.

To Kim Campbell for your editing and picking up on all my mistakes. You truly are amazing.

And lastly to you readers. Thank you so much for taking the time to read my book. I hope you enjoyed it and I can't wait to hear what you think.

Until next time

Kristen

x

Follow Me

I would love to hear from you!

You would seriously make my day if you got in contact with me on my social media pages.

You can find me on Facebook – Author Kristen Dovnik. I'm on here quiet regularly.

I'm also on Instagram – authorkristendovnik
I'm frequently on here.

And for those of you who do not have social media you can find me at my website. www.kristendovnik.com

I hope to hear from you soon
X

Author Bio

Kristen loves to write just as much as she loves to read. For years, she's imagined wonderful characters and exciting storylines, just waiting, waiting to be brought to life. Now that her children are a little older, she has the time to enjoy her passion for writing and is putting pen to paper, giving life to her characters and stories.

Kristen resides in Sydney, Australia with her husband Robby, and three very energetic, young children. She loves nothing more than spending time with her family or sitting down with a slice of vegemite toast, a good cup of coffee and writing the next exciting chapter for her characters.

www.ingramcontent.com/pod-product-compliance
Lightning Source LLC
Chambersburg PA
CBHW020912310726
48980CB00011B/852/J

* 9 7 8 0 6 4 8 9 5 4 0 9 5 *